D0820373

Karma
and Other Stories

Karma
and Other Stories

Susan Dunlap

DEC 2002
CONTRA COSTA COUNTY LIBRARY

Five Star • Waterville, Maine

3 1901 03178 5613

Copyright © 2002 by Susan Dunlap

All stories reprinted by permission of the author.

"The Court of Celestial Appeals," copyright © 1996 by Susan Dunlap. First published in *Guilty as Charged*.

"A Contest Fit for a Queen," copyright © 1995 by Susan Dunlap. First published in *Crimes of the Heart*.

Karma, copyright © 1981 by Susan Dunlap.

All rights reserved.

This collection is a work of fiction. Names, characters, places, and incidents are either the product of the author's imagination, or, if real, used fictitiously.

Five Star First Edition Mystery Series.

Published in 2002 in conjunction with Tekno-Books and Ed Gorman.

Set in 11 pt. Plantin by Elena Picard.

Printed in the United States on permanent paper.

Library of Congress Cataloging-in-Publication Data

Dunlap, Susan.
    Karma and other stories / Susan Dunlap.
      p. cm.—(Five Star first edition mystery series)
    Contents: The Court of Celestial Appeals—A contest fit for a queen—Karma.
    ISBN 0-7862-4173-X (hc : alk. paper)
    1. Detective and mystery stories, American. I. Title.
II. Series.
PS3554.U46972 K37 2002
  813'.54—dc21   2002025171

Table of Contents

The Court of Celestial Appeals

Death is not all it's cracked up to be.

Heaven or Hell, or the forty days and nights traveling through the *Bardo* to the next incarnation? Limbo, Purgatory, or a return to the elements from which the body came? I wouldn't have bet my life on the location of my eternal domicile, but I assumed at least I would recognize the place when I got there.

But this? It's like waking up in another beige hotel room in another overcast city; you can't remember where you are or why you're there. For a moment you don't know who you are. I remember that feeling in . . . but the city's gone. Of course.

I'm gone.

I don't know who I am, or was. Or where I am. Or why I'm here. I just know I'm dead. And I've been summoned back to the Court of Final Appeals, for the third time. There's a lot I don't know about this place, but I do know that in this court, the third time is not a charm.

The halls are all off-white here. They glow a little, but not as gaudily as the near-death books suggest—no blinding white light at the end of every corridor and—thank God—no powerful suction toward it. Moving down a corridor is hard enough as it is when you've got wings.

Actually, the wings were the first disappointment. To fly! I loved it. I raced down the hall, veering left, scraping the wall, correcting, over-correcting, ignoring the rasping pain on my wing edge, caught up in anticipation of that wonderful moment of take-off. But the snack machine room at the end of the corridor came first. I turned, banging a wing into the ambrosia dispenser, and raced full-out down the hall. No luck.

It wasn't till I saw the Sub-Authority, that I accepted the humbling truth. In this place we only fly in the sense that penguins fly. Sort of a scurry and bounce. It's most appealing to those deceased meditationists who see it as levitating and take their newfound ability as a sign of enlightenment.

They're not in danger of arriving unprepared for a third Hearing in the Court of Final Appeals.

I should be spending my time researching my case, but . . . I play a little game. It involves twisting one of the Celestial Rules. The Rules aren't shouted out over a loudspeaker like specials in the supermarket: "Attention Dead Shoppers! Ultra Gold Halo Cleaner on aisle six! Snap it up while the supply lasts!" There are no proclamations, no notices posted. Here, things are just known. One of those "things" is that you are forbidden to open the doors along the corridor. No reason for the "Off Limits." The Boss doesn't need to give out His rationale. And it seems superfluous to ask the punishment.

But few things are so seductive as a closed door. A closed *unlocked* door. There's a reason temptation has maintained its appeal all these centuries.

So I try a handle now and then. It's how I learned there are worse places to spend eternity than the white corridor.

In my first peek, I just about killed myself (or I would have if I hadn't already been dead) checking up and down the corridor for spies. Finally, not so much reassured as impatient, I inched open the door and found myself in a room that contained another world. Outdoors. San Francisco. And I was standing on the railing of the fly over that merges into the Bay Bridge. Traffic was backed up far as the eye could see (and one thing you get up here is 20-20). Rain bombarded the idling cars; the sky was five o'clock dark. A broken-down semi blocked the inner lane and traffic squeezed into the remaining lane. Half a mile back, cars from the on-ramp to the right had merged in, too. The surviving line of vehicles inched forward. A yellow Volkswagen bug puttered along in the lane, the driver's face rush-hour tight. A big blue Chevy pick-up raced along the shoulder. The driver should have merged into the VW's lane half a mile back. His lane had petered out. It was now-or-never for him. He slowed, veered closer to inching cars, eyeing each one predatorily until he spotted the little VW bug. He pounced left, barely missing the fragile bumper as the bug's brakes squealed. *Volkswagen Hell!* I thought. But just then, the Volkswagen driver hit his horn, an air horn loud enough to wake the . . . well . . . dead. And to terrify the pick-up driver. He swerved into the guardrail. Ah. *Volkswagen Heaven!*

The pick-up driver leapt from his wrinkled vehicle, turned to glare. And came face to face with a Highway Patrol officer. Not just Volkswagen Heaven but *Pick-up Hell!*

The pick-up driver could have pocketed his ticket and exited his Hell. He could have walked right out through the door with me. Instead, he leapt angrily into the driver's seat, screeched back, shifted into first, gunned the engine and found himself where he had started, a mile back on the entry ramp, and desperate to try to cut the line again, eternally.

I backed out into my hallway, shut the door and spun around with a second to spare before the Sub-Authority glided down the corridor. Had he spotted me? He didn't let on. But coincidences rarely occur up here.

I should have clutched my close call to my breast that day

and never turned another doorknob. A wise person would have.

A wise person would be in Heaven.

Doors became my life, so to speak. I "lived" to lurk, to sidle, to snoop. Held breath, panicked gasps became my norm of respiration. I tried every door on the corridor, every corridor that crossed mine. I turned right and left, checking for spies till my wings were rubbed bare. The Sub-Authority never returned. I don't know when it struck me that the coast was always clear. I was the only real person on the corridor. It was then that I had the worst thought: that someone else might be sneaking open a door on a more rarified corridor, looking down and spotting me peering into forbidden rooms, eternally.

But now the call has come; they have pounced. The Boss frowns on dawdling when He's called you to court. If I thought there was any chance of escaping it, I would dawdle eternally. The Court of *Final* Appeals.

Like all the dead, I had had my day—*days*—in court when I arrived. The time of endless appeals is long gone up here. Once the Boss decides, who's to appeal to? That's one thing you know when you arrive. Not that it makes your initiation any easier.

Some of the newly dead—we call them *Cools*—have solid expectations of what this place should look like and how the Boss should handle things. Many expect to see their own face or similar ones on all around. They all expect the Boss to resemble themselves.

If they survived long enough to outlive friends and relatives, they expect the Dear Departed to be assembled and waiting anxiously. Not just rounded up, but on their best behavior, in many cases better behavior than they ever exhibited on earth. In the mind of the Cool the cousin he cheated, left destitute, and pushed into suicide, will not merely have forgiven him. That cousin will not have forgotten the event, but instead will see the Cool's motivation in a new light. He will, in fact, be eager to admit that he was wrong and it was the Cool who was the true victim. He'll be pushing in front of the Dear Departed to beat his breast and open his arms.

No other evidence need be shown to prove how quickly Cools forget life below. They expect the rest of those waiting relatives to be holding out hands toward them, comforting them after their traumatic experience, waiting anxiously for their first words. They never picture cousins bored, uncles scarfing beers and dozing off in armchairs, and aunts too busy quarreling to be bothered with them.

But explicit as their expectations are, almost invariably the Cools' ideas of the Final Hearing are vague. They mutter about sheep and goats as if the Hearing—the only real thing among their fairy tale expectations—is all Brothers Grimm.

I don't know what I expected from my own Final Hearing, but what I found was certainly not it.

My first misapprehension was architectural. No way would I have guessed that the design of the Celestial Hearing Chamber would be based on the municipal court in Contra Costa County, California. Not even Superior Court! But there it was, a room paneled in middling wood, a judge's bench, and on the wall a gold disk about four feet across.

There is a bailiff—not in the ill-fitting tans of below, but in an off-white robe (straight out of the movies). "All rise," he calls. "The honorable Sub-Authority presiding." It's a bit of show, since no one but the Cool is in the room, and he's much too nervous to sit.

The bailiff reads the charges. He lists every trespass in deed, in word (and in words Cools assumed were whispered in confidence, not recorded for the ears of the heavenly host), and worst of all, the bailiff delineates, rather too lovingly, every transgression in thought. I mean, who would have thought . . .

The list goes on . . . and on . . . and on. It's the first time the Cool realizes what's meant by eternity. There may, in the fullness of time, be worse moments, and longer ones. I doubt it. Hours, days, eons pass; his knees quiver like earthquakes, floods of sweat deluge his body, his eyes glaze over, and the synapses in his brain fire off in a war of their own. And when the list finally ends, and the Cool is reduced to a little formless blob of fear, the Sub-Authority looks him straight in the eye, pauses, and pronounces: "All is forgiven."

All is forgiven!

You would think the Cool would be ecstatic, right? Some are. Some inhale that forgiveness like oxygen into the lungs of the suffocating; they smile sheepishly, humbly, amazedly, clutch their clean slates to their breasts, and then, as if afraid the Sub-Authority might realize his mistake, they race through the great double doors that lead to—But that *I* don't—cannot—know.

Some Cools accept the gift with grace. But not most. Most are, well, suspicious. To accept forgiveness for oneself is one thing, to sign on to clemency for *all* is another matter entirely. Just how all encompassing was that divine pardon, they want to know. *I* wanted to know. Then their court-appointed lawyer asks for a continuance to the next day. The Sub-Authority granted *my* continuance, and my lawyer took me out in the hall, gave me a videotape of my transgressions and said: "Go over that tape and think about how lucky you are."

I did.

The next day I arrived back in court. The procedure was repeated. I knew I should have taken the offer—most people do by this stage, con men and crooks faster than the rest—

they're used to playing the odds, and they know when those odds are not likely to improve. But I couldn't accept it. I don't know why. I wish I did. I would give a lot to know why. But, here, I have nothing to give.

My lawyer glared down the length of his nose at me, and asked for another continuance. The Sub-Authority's face pulled into a similarly un-angelic expression. But in the end he shrugged and granted the delay.

This time when my lawyer took me out into the hallway the very air was colder, thicker against my ribs. Each panicked breath smacked my ribs against the air; every beat of my heart hurt—phantom pain of phantom heart, but all too real panic. My lawyer's voice rasped my ears as he said, "You know what Three Strikes means?"

"When am I out?"

"Tomorrow, if you don't wise up and take the offer."

"And if I can't?"

He shook his head, smacked his wings tight against his scapulae, and glided way.

So I pace, up one corridor, down the next, hoping as I come to the intersections, that I'll turn the corner on my own problem and be whisked back to the final, triumphant hearing, and then on to . . . well, on to something so superbly wonderful it defies description.

Since then, I've opened a lot of closed doors, seen many things that shocked me, but none more than the scene inside the room marked 'Please Do Not Enter.'

I inched the door open and stood peering in on the Sub-Authority himself in his ostentatiously simple robe, thin lips pulled back in a scowl, glaring down his chiseled Puritan nose at a memo.

And facing him was the one Personage powerful enough to tell him No. All powerful. All knowing. All seeing.

Quickly, I slid behind the door.

It was then that I heard the Sub-Authority saying, "Can't stay here, Your Selfness."

It was *me* he was talking about.

"The corridor is for temporary stays, the occasional *one* night lodging for extremely indecisive and extremely *rare* souls."

I stuck my head beyond the doorframe in time to see him shaking that memo impatiently.

I held my breath. Surely the Great Personage would come to my support. If this wasn't the time to demonstrate All Lovingness, what was?

But it was the Sub-Authority who spoke. "They all choose by the third hearing. The third hearing is *always* within a day of the second. This one" —I cringed—"has been stalling for longer than that already. This one is no closer to decision now than upon entry." His fingers tightened around the memo.

I strained to hear the reply. The Sub-Authority's jaw tightened; his fingers clenched into a fist. Dammit, if I could just get closer and *hear* . . . It was then I realized it wouldn't have mattered how close I was. I could have been standing between them. The voice of the Boss is never *heard*. He doesn't communicate in words.

"That one," the Sub-Authority countered, "has been spotted breaking the rules. What we've got here is a troublemaker. A troublemaker who cannot decide to go on and cannot keep the nose out of other penitent's business while here. Take that into account, your Selfness. Make the judgment. Send that one down."

My whole soul went cold. I wanted to rush into the room, throw myself at the Authority's feet—if He had feet—and scream, "I'll take the forgiveness. Please don't send me down. I'll forgive anyone—*all*."

But, even with the smell of brimstone rank in my nostrils, I couldn't. I just couldn't bring myself to. I folded my wings tight against my back and prepared for descent.

The Sub-Authority inhaled sharply and leaned forward, both hands shaking angrily. "But, Sir, we can't justify making an exception so unprecedented, not for this one."

My wings relaxed a scintilla.

"I know it's an important job," he admitted. "Admittedly this one has shown abnormal aptitude for the work. I suppose we *could* suspend the rules if the job is performed to satisfaction. But one failure and it's—" He glanced abruptly down, the hint of a smile on his face. In a moment the smile broadened.

And the door slammed shut.

I stood in the icy corridor. Damn, why couldn't I have accepted the forgiveness? Why? What could have been so terrible that I couldn't forgive it, even at the cost of my own eternal damnation? I strained, but not one image came to mind. Even under such extreme pressure I couldn't recall who I was, much less what had happened to me.

If I didn't figure out how to remember I was going to be in deep brimstone. But I had no idea how to go about it.

After that, the one thing you'd have expected of me was good behavior. You would assume I'd never have peered through another door. But, somehow the tenuousness of my position made me dart around more rashly than before. I felt like a gourmand sworn to start a diet in the morning, an alcoholic drinking his last bottle of scotch. It was that same day I came upon the pick-up driver on the Bay Bridge.

So, you see, I know how the Cools feel. Most of them go over and over that tape the first night, reliving some of the transgressing deeds they enjoyed entirely too much, shuddering at the anti-social thoughts that had sailed through their minds as if sent by a sociopath. By that second day they jump at the Hearing offer and nearly trip themselves running through the great double doors.

But the man at this trial . . .

I realized now I wasn't just *remembering* but was actually *at* a new trial. Time is funny here.

The defendant at today's trial was shaking his head, when his lawyer asked for not a continuance—under the rules he couldn't do that at that point—but a short recess.

Then he turned to me and said, "He can't make up his mind. He doesn't have a clue. He knows *how* he died, but he can't move on till he finds out *why* he died. You're the detective, you hunt that down."

"How am I going to—"

"My client doesn't have time for chatter. We're only recessed till after lunch. (The lawyer almost smiled. Up here we hardly 'do lunch.' There is no Food-For-The-Soul Cafe, no Veal Valhalla, no fresh greens from the Garden of the Hesperides.) He's waiting for you in the hall."

What does a detective do? There had to be some job qualifications besides nosiness. Had I been a detective in life? I sure didn't picture myself as a pre-mortem gumshoe. How do you start an investigation, particularly when the subject is up here and the facts are down there? If I were such a natural detective I'd have been able to find out why I died myself instead of wandering around baffled up here.

A flash of anger shot through me. They expected me to find out how he died when *I* had died and no one had been assigned to do it for *me!* The hell to them! I'd refuse. A celestial sit-down strike. If they didn't like it they could—

An acrid whiff of brimstone cut through the bland air.

Then it occurred to me that I had a chance here. There was time on the off-white hallway to peek into rooms; why couldn't I make time in this investigation for my own search? Hundreds of thousands of people died every day; hundreds of thousands of trials go on simultaneously. As I headed out to this job the Sub-Authority would have plenty to worry about besides my time card. I'd just need to keep an eye out for my chance.

I walked slowly out the door and glanced at the defendant on the bench, sitting there within moments of the possibility of eternal damnation. He was a tidy, lightly-tanned Caucasian male of middle age, wearing an expensive blue pinstriped suit with lines so subtle I almost missed them, and a maroon silk handkerchief in his pocket. His hair was still dark, and despite his age no looseness of skin marred the firm, square line of his jaw. And his expression—had I considered the possibilities beforehand I might have expected fear or remorse—was one of outrage.

"You people have made a mistake!" he said by way of introduction.

"Wha—" I let out before I caught myself. *You people,* indeed. What did I look like, a sub Sub-Authority? I was offended. And shocked at how offended I was. And at how quickly I realized there was protective cover in this new role of mine.

I settled next to him on the wooden bench and restrained the urge to say: "A mistake? Ah, they all say that, Mr. Girard." Humor is so unappreciated in this place. There are times I think the real reason people are kept here at all is they are insufficiently venal to be sent below and too dull to be tolerated above. The Boss, after all, has to live up there. It's probably why He keeps the Sub-Authority down here.

I glanced over at Charles Girard, noting with some surprise how well he suited the name I hadn't known till a moment ago. "Mr. Girard, up here all things are possible. We can make whatever He wants. Mistakes are not one of those things."

He opened his mouth to protest. The words seemed to hover at the outlet of his lips. "How could this happen to me?"

"How could *what* happen to you?"

"The bit—woman killed me!"

"Well, something had to." The moment the words left my lips I knew they were a mistake. Again I wondered why had I been chosen a celestial detective—obviously not for my tact. "Start at the beginning with your name."

"Stone Girard," he said as if it were a household word.

"Stone?"

"Nickname. Had it for years."

"Because you did drugs?"

God, why did I keep poking at the man? He was hardly the type I could picture sprawled with a hookah or hypodermic. Nor, I gathered from the raise of his eyebrows, and the angry clamp of his jaw, could he. "Never! I never broke the law!"

"Let me remind you where you are, Stone. Up here you are always under oath."

It was a moment before he regained enough composure to insist, "Never once did I knowingly break the law."

"Knowingly? Ah hah!" Having to tell the truth, that's a shock for a lot of them. In some cases it leaves them nothing to say. Stone was being honest, if not helpful. And I could hardly ask him what law it was that he didn't know he'd broken.

"*I* would hardly have broken the law," he insisted as if he'd read my mind. "I was a judge."

In a great show of control, I said nothing.

"And I was running for the United States Senate!"

I couldn't help it; I laughed. "Senator from—?"

"California."

Another laugh escaped. California, the bastion of political frivolity. That state whose citizens viewed sending politicians to Washington as civil comic relief. They prided themselves on delivering to statehouse and D.C. the flashy, the weird, the nascent politicians with more dollars than sense, victors who became known as Teflon or Moonbeam, losers who refused to admit defeat till a third of a year after the vote. Californians tended toward high comedy, spiritual eccentricity, or façade. They had never raised political corruption to the art form of states like New Jersey, where city councils could have had quorums behind bars. But dishonesty was not unknown in the Golden State. I considered whether Stone's protest was indicative of remarkable naiveté, and decided that he merely meant a gubernatorial candidate was wise to be circumspect. Stone clutched a bunch of newspapers and shook them at me. The rustling of the pages grated oddly on my ears. The breeze chilled my bald head. It's so warm up here I'd almost forgotten why the still-living have hair. "I'm not—I *wasn't*," Stone said, "one of those political idiots who can't keep it zipped." He smacked the papers into my hand.

That he still had the papers didn't surprise me. Death is such a loss. To lose a loved one can be hard. But when that loved one is the one you hold most dear—yourself—it gives *hard* new meaning. Cools come across kicking and screaming and clinging on for dear life. Literally. To calm them, the Sub-Authority offers them a last look below. An invisible box seat at the event of their choice. Some of the Cools who join us in January choose to see the football playoff games. Artists up for awards, scientists in the running for grants often choose to see the ceremonies. Parents opt for views of children's graduations. The occasional charismatic leader needs to see who his followers chose to succeed him.

But far and away the most popular event for a Cool is his

funeral—the one time he is the true and deserving center of attention. A Cool may hate the idea of being up here, but the offer of a bird's-eye view of his wake is more than most can pass up. Cools love the sobbers and the bawlers wailing as if their old hearts would break. They cherish the priestly eulogies extolling their noble natures, embellishing their wit, exaggerating their generosity. They clutch to their now formless breasts their friends' sincere emotions unspoken in life. Equally do they treasure their enemies' counterfeit grief, the "loving memories," the panoplies of insincere praise those enemies have no choice but to choke out. Richard Nixon just about fell off his chair in the viewing room. I hadn't realized the man had such a sense of humor.

The Sub-Authority allows that. He doesn't object to the Cool clinging to a newspaper account of the event.

But three papers—that was a bit much.

I looked down at the top one so summarily smacked in my hand. Stone Girard was a well-known man. His death was not an addendum in the obit column. It was front-page news.

"Girard Dead at Lovers Leap!" the *Los Angeles Times* screamed in a banner headline.

"Girard Found Dead with Mystery Woman," the *San Francisco Chronicle* proclaimed.

"Political Fall: Same Old Story," the *Bay Guardian* shook its printed head. "If Stone Girard had taken stock of himself before he threw his hat in the ring, he wouldn't had felt obligated to toss the rest of himself onto the Great Highway. If Girard couldn't wait till after the election to take up with Olivia Cummings, what his choice tells us is California is left with the better man."

Marc Bellingham, by default the senate-elect presumptive, clearly understood the better part of valor. From the length of the headline article Bellingham was the only one within the Golden State or the United States Senate who did not have a comment on Girard's passing.

I read the coverage in all three papers and every one of the comments. And while the word *stupid* was never employed, and no one recalled Gary Hart and his sailboat per se, I doubted there was a euphemism in the English language that had gone unused, nor any two lines that could not be read between. The closest reporters came to censoring the defunct candidate was denigrating his choice of leap, from an outcropping of rock above the Great Highway. If Girard hadn't died in the fall he'd have been crushed by a tourist bus. Stone Girard may have been, as he had insisted to me a minute earlier, "not one of those political idiots who can't keep it zipped." But his way of departure was unlikely to garner him the epitaph of political visionary.

"Mr. Girard—"

"Stone."

"Stone, you and Olivia Cummings were found dead, *together,* at the bottom of Sutro Heights promontory."

Girard pulled his tidy form up to his full, if not impressive, height. "Don't even suggest that I was philandering. I am a man of principle. I did not entertain assignations. I wasn't called Stone for nothing."

Repressing a smile, I asked, "Why were you called Stone, Stone?"

"Because, young . . ." Stone assessed my hairless pate, swept his eyes discreetly down the front of my robe, apparently unaware that the soul is without sexual indicators. "My detractors called me Stone because I was sufficiently upright to cast the first one. They aimed to make me a laughing stock, but I wasn't laughing—"

That I believed. I'd yet to see any indication Stone Girard had a sense of humor. He had the makings of the Sub-

Authority's right-hand man.

"—I took that name and made it my slogan. Voters want a man they can trust. They want to vote for a man who could cast the first stone. Bellingham may scoff at purity, but I'll tell you, little . . . person . . . these days purity is a plus."

"But, Stone, your body was found with this woman. How do you explain that?"

His jaw quivered. "I don't know."

"You don't know?"

"No, dammit, I have no idea."

I started to retort, then backed off. Maybe he was being truthful. His chiseled face was hewn into an expression of bewilderment. If so, it was no wonder he couldn't come to a decision at his Hearing.

Newly arrived Cools have no memory of the day of their death. Death can be traumatic, and Judgment is no piece of cake either. Particularly for those who've spent their lives pretending they are the Boss' earthly representatives. The Cools have plenty to contemplate without recalling their dying days. Memory blackout is a good rule, but it was going to make my job harder. "Okay, Stone, for now we'll skip the reason for your presence on Sutro Heights. Tell me about the woman. Who was Olivia Cummings?"

"Nobody."

"Hardly nobody, Stone. Au contraire, not just a body but a corpus delicti. Was she an old flame?"

"No, no, no. I barely knew the woman. She was married to someone else."

"Are you sure?"

"Of course, I am. I married her myself."

A grin pulled at my lips.

"When I was a judge, I performed the ceremony. My one and only marriage."

"How come no more?"

He shot glances in both directions of the hallway, then lowering his voice, said, "I wouldn't want this to become public—"

"Don't worry. The old adage that the cemeteries vote democrat isn't true. There are no absentee ballots from here."

He flushed, then his eyes widened in horror. I had the feeling that for the first time he was really taking in the fact that he didn't have to worry about the election.

"You gave up performing marriages because—" I prompted.

"They take a lot of time and a judge can't accept payment for them. California Penal Code section ninety-four point five."

"Why not, so the judge can't be bribed?"

"It doesn't matter whether the payment was intended as a bribe or not. No money, no thing of value. Not before the wedding, not after."

"A judge can't be paid ever?"

"Not unless the wedding is performed on a Saturday, Sunday, or holiday."

"California, Land of Loopholes!" I threw my head back and laughed so hard my wings flapped. I nearly flung myself into the wall.

Stone cleared his throat, magistratively.

"Okay," I said, shifting my wings back in place. "But you did perform this one marriage, Olivia Cummings' wedding. Why?"

"It was a spur of the moment thing. They just called me because I was handy."

"Can you clarify that?" That sounded bland and legal enough for Stone.

"Olivia's father called me because I was spending the weekend in the other half of their cottage in Tahoe."

Cottage in this case could be a euphemism worthy of Stone's wake. "How big a cottage?"

"I don't know, three, four bedrooms."

"Who was Olivia's father?"

"Avery Cummings."

"Avery Cummings, the shipping magnate?"

"I don't know."

"Stone, remember where you are. The truth?"

"Cummings owned some ships."

"How many?"

"I don't—the Pan Asia Line."

I smiled to myself. Maybe I *was* cut out for this job. If the cases were all this easy, it'd be a snap. At this rate I would have plenty of time to check up on my own demise. "And so Stone, afterwards Avery Cummings supported your political campaign, right?"

"Wrong."

"The truth, remember?"

Girard jutted out his chin. "Cummings never gave me a dime. Never promised a loan or twisted an arm."

"He supported your opponent?"

"Him neither. Took no sides in politics. Said it didn't matter who won, nothing changed. Sounded like a goddamned radical. Said the best political investment for him was keeping his money in his pocket. And that's just what he did."

Surely not. I tried again, "But he let you use his vacation house."

"Let me *rent* it, at the going rate."

Okay, so the banker didn't go out of his way. But his daughter's wedding—half the money in California could have been invited. A couple of well-placed introductions and Stone could have been set for his whole campaign. "But at the wedding, he did introduce you to his influential friends, right?"

"He introduced me to his scatter-brained daughter, his cotton-headed son-in-law-to-be, and the maid and gardener he called in to be witnesses."

"And—?"

"That's all. No one else was there. They had to drag the maid out of bed. And the gardener. The guy didn't live on the grounds—we're just talking a house here, sizeable, but not an estate. The gardener lived in a cabin ten miles into the woods. Cummings called the guy's brother in town, got him up, convinced him to drive out to the guy's cabin and bring him back."

"Convinced him how?" I said, perking up.

"Financially," Stone said in the tone he'd have used with a particularly dim-witted lawyer.

But I wasn't about to be deterred, not when I knew the consequences of his being recompensed. "Did you hear him offer the gardener cash?"

"It was understood."

"Ah-ha!"

"What does that mean?" he demanded icily.

"That you, too, could expect him to make it worth your while."

"I didn't! *He* didn't. Expect it or receive a cent from him. He didn't give me the benefit of his influence. He never once contributed to a campaign of mine. I don't think the man voted at all. And his damned daughter gave a couple thou to Bellingham. In fact, the whole affair ended up costing me."

"Costing you?"

"Right. I slept through a nine a.m. meeting I'd scheduled

with Donald Davis, the financier. Davis was a potential contributor. With all the shenanigans connected with the wedding, the miserable affair took half the night. The groom was so drunk Cummings had to throw him in the shower to sober him up. Then Olivia decided she'd made the right decision when she called off the formal wedding—it was scheduled for a couple of weeks later—and flounced off to bed. If I'd been smart I'd have hightailed it out of there."

"But you didn't?"

"No. Big mistake. Cummings asked me to have a brandy with him, to settle us both down after the fiasco of an evening. So he pours the brandy and we're sitting there, and out comes the son-in-law-to-be. By now he's alert enough to realize he's been jilted for a second time and he's prowling the house, moaning like a dog with a churning stomach. I wanted to force some bicarb down his jaw and tie him to a stake in the yard."

I glanced at Stone's face to see if he intended to be amusing. Nothing suggested so.

"I just sat with Cummings, sipping the brandy. Sat silent. Just calming down. Should have kept watch on the son-in-law. Boy must have groaned his way down the hall to the girl's room. Must have made her sorry enough or horny enough to reconsider. Whatever. I was just about out the door when the two of them came racing in, grinning ear to ear, announcing they'd changed their minds."

"What about the gardener?" The question had nothing to do with the answers I needed, but I was too caught up in the story not to wonder about the groggy gardener and his groggy brother and the cabin ten miles into the woods.

"He was still at his brother's. It had started to rain about midnight and he'd decided not to make the trip back to his own cabin. So Cummings called a cab for him. When he got there, I lined 'em up, performed the ceremony—the actual legal necessities don't take long—and was back in my half of the cottage before the groom had kissed the bride." He shook his head. "Got myself so soaked I had to take a hot bath. Probably the reason I overslept, snubbed Davis, teed him off, basically kicked him into the other camp. Almost lost the election because of it. Davis has big bucks." He hesitated, glanced around furtively, then said, "Or at least he did. Dead now. Is he . . ."

"They all come through here, Stone. Where they go after I can't say."

"Not in the loop, eh?"

"Can't say," I managed to get out in a neutral tone. Of course, I didn't know what had become of money-man Davis. The Sub-Authority doesn't report to me on the disposal of souls. But I wasn't about to admit that to Stone. Much less was I willing to show my pique. Up here, they frown on pique.

The smell of brimstone wafted past my nose. I shot a glance behind me, but, of course, there was no fire, not yet. Whatever the source of that evil smell, it did snap my attention back to the vital task at hand. Fail to solve Stone's dilemma and I would have eternity to contemplate the fate of Davis. Maybe he'd be right down there next to me, fanning the flames. "What became of Olivia and her groom?"

If Stone said they had a storybook marriage, topped by three charming children, all Rhodes scholars, I would have been surprised.

I wasn't.

"Divorced. Marriage lasted fifteen years. I would've put money on less than one. I'm not often wrong."

"But you were this time." I grinned.

"True. Figure it took Oren that long to run through Olivia's money. No pre-nuptial agreement. Doesn't surprise

27

me. They didn't plan anything else, why would they all of a sudden get responsibility and think about that?"

"Surely old man Cummings, a banker, would have pressed for it."

"You didn't know Olivia. Stubborn as she was spoiled and self-centered. Thought the world owed her a living. Figured as long as there was a world she'd go on living high. As for old man Cummings, he must have decided it wasn't worth the fight to buck Olivia on this. He was only in his fifties at the time. He must have figured he'd long out-live the marriage."

"Didn't he?"

"Nope. Heart attack the next year. That's why Oren and Olivia stayed married as long as they did. If they hadn't had her inheritance to go through they would have seen each other in the cold light of dawn a lot sooner. But money and illegal substances can rose-color the worst of situations."

"So they divorced?"

"Three years ago. Oren's a viper, but he's got a certain reptilian charm. Married more money within the year. Lives on an estate in Hillsborough."

"And Olivia?"

"Not so fortunate. High living took its toll. She was one of those chipmunk-faced girls kept from being plain by youth and money. Without either she came to resemble a Basset."

I shivered for Olivia; rolls of skin are more appealing on the face of an exotic dog than a matron. "So what did she do for money?"

"Hit up everyone she knew. It was embarrassing. I mean how sorry can you be for a whiny woman who's run through a couple mil? Oh, some friends of the family helped out. An aunt gave her a studio in the city. A cousin took her by the scruff of the neck and explained the facts of life."

"Like?"

"Work! Said he'd pay for her to take classes. Para-legal, it turned out. Olivia made it through a semester, maybe two. But when you expect the world to support you, work isn't part of the plan. Dropped out."

"And then?"

He shook his head. "Heard not a thing about her till she called. Yesterday." Girard paled. "God, just yesterday I was . . . alive."

"Don't think about that! You don't have time. Not now. *Olivia!* What happened after she called?"

She had arranged to meet him at Sutro Heights. Because all that happened the day of his death, he wouldn't remember it. He wouldn't know why he went, or what happened. Maybe she was so enraged he'd gotten her married to Oren in the first place that she pushed him over the cliff. Or perhaps he saw her in a new and seductive light, reached passionately for her and together they slipped into oblivion.

I didn't picture Stone rushing to an amorous tryst with a whiny, vindictive woman who looked like a low-slung hound. Certainly not the week before the election. No way would Stone Girard set up a clandestine meeting at a lover's leap with a woman of questionable reputation.

Still, he did.

I started to ask him, more pointedly, what possessed him. But before I could speak he faded into the off-white wall.

"Get back here!" I yelled.

No response.

I banged my fist in fury, but it's a waste of time in a room where there's nothing solid to hit. "Hey," I yelled into the atmosphere where the Sub-Authority was probably lurking, "this is really unfair. If you expect me to investigate, you've got to give me access to my client!"

No reaction at all.

"You know what kind of deal this is? Huh? A diabolical one!" That's a big insult, but not big enough to draw the Sub-Authority out. Clearly, I'd gotten all I was going to from Stone Girard. I hoped it was all I needed.

Once again fetors of brimstone rasped against my nose. No time for anger. I had to think. I coasted back and forth in front of the courtroom door. Why do people kill? Love. None of that lost here. Hate. Stone and Olivia were too inconsequential to each other. Envy, jealousy, revenge, greed—Ah, greed. Blackmail. One of the few ways of income acquisition left for Olivia. The conclusion quite pleased me.

Until her lack struck me. What had she blackmailed him with? The man had merely done her a kindness. Still, blackmail was all Olivia Cummings had left. But facts I didn't have.

What I did have, I realized, was one chance to peruse the evidence in person. I could choose my scene and go below, back to the time and be there as it occurred. One scene, but only one.

I'd take the minute before he died.

No, I wouldn't. The time he'd blocked out was blacked out for me, too. I had to travel through *his* memory. Somehow from all the minutes and hours in his life, I had to pick out the key moment. If I didn't . . . but I was already sick of brimstone.

Rain dripped down my neck, soft as if the drops broke their falls just before they landed on my skin, caressingly cool against the warm humid late summer air. The fresh and pure scent of an incense cedar cut the smell of wet grass. In the distance cars accelerated on the dark, empty stretch of road behind Cummings' Tahoe duplex roaring in quickening passion, gasping for breath, for gear change, speeding faster to a climax out of my hearing. Whiffs of gasoline came and were gone. In the shock of silence that followed, the gentle lapping of the lake seemed to pound like tsunamis.

Cummings' house was everything I might have imagined: large, shingled, the living space secluded from roadside eyes. Standing ten feet off the path by the front door, I watched as the portal opened. Stone stalked out. Face pinched, breath heaving angrily, his ire focused on a foot high glass jade plant in his hands. He stalked across the wet lawn toward the other door, *his* door, soft leather shoes squishing in the mud. He barely noticed that, so intent was he on stripping off the small glass leaves of the jade plant, one after another, and pitching them in the bushes. "A leaf for every damned minute!" he grumbled as he tossed the last one against the shingles, and fingered his pocket for the door key. "Some 'thank you.' "

He stepped inside.

I could feel myself fading. I couldn't be pulled back yet! I hadn't solved Girard's death, and hadn't even thought about my own demise! I couldn't go back up there with nothing! I curled my toes, trying to clutch the earth, to wrap myself around the smell of the cedar, sound of the icy lake water splatting on the shore. Of earth. I hadn't realized how much I missed it. Greedily I moved my gaze back and forth over the sky, the clouds, the trees, the lawn imprinting them all on my memory. The pull grew stronger, a budding tornado in reverse.

On the road a horn blew.

I slipped behind a redwood, raced to the bushes, stooping low behind them. Sweat coated my neck. I inched toward Girard's front door, hoping he'd been too distracted to lock it. The wind, the *pull,* sucked the fallen leaves off the grass, twisted the fronds of the redwoods. I reached for the doorknob and was inside.

In a vestibule with a closet, mirror, narrow table and a book, *The Perfect Crime*, by Leigh Ward. I grabbed it and slid into the safety of the closet.

The hallway outside the courtroom was empty, no Cools, no staff, no smells, not even a familiar soundless word. Footsteps came down the hall toward me, slowly, from a distance. Stone's steps. When he reached me, we would go into the courtroom, he would turn to me, then he'd have to give his answer.

Stone paused next to me, reached for the double door and we walked in. The great seal gleamed down at us. From under it the Sub-Authority exhaled slowly. "Charles Stone Girard, all is forgiven. Do you accept forgiveness for all?"

Stone turned to me.

I pictured the pick-up driver in the room on the corridor, trying to cut the line, smashing into the railing, getting the ticket, and starting over again, endlessly, blocking out reality with his insistence. Stone was a judge. He should have known what was in the penal code. Laws can be foolish, but only a fool ignores them, particularly if he's running for senate. Only a fool drives into the same railing again and again. Only a fool assumes a jade plant is so insufficient a "thank you" as to be of no value at all.

I said, "California Penal Code section ninety-four point five." The code appeared in his hand:

Acceptance of fee by judicial officer for performance of marriage. Every judge, justice, commissioner, or assistant commissioner of a court of this state who accepts any money or other thing of value for performing any marriage, including any money or thing of value voluntarily tendered by the persons about to be married or who have been married by such judge etc whether the acceptance occurs before or after performance of the marriage and whether or not performance of a marriage is conditioned on the giving of such money or the thing of value by the persons being married is guilty of a misdemeanor.

It is not a necessary element of the offense described by this section that the acceptance of the money or other thing of value be committed with intent to commit extortion or with other criminal intent.

This section does not apply to an acceptance of a fee for performing a marriage of Saturday, Sunday, or a legal holiday.

"And section ninety-eight:"

Officers to forfeit and be disqualified from holding office. Every officer convicted of any crime defined in this chapter, in addition to the punishment described, forfeits his office and is forever disqualified from holding any office in this state.

It was a moment before Stone groaned. "You mean the fucking jade plant? I could lose the Senate seat because of that jade plant?"

I nodded.

His shoulders slumped, he started to sag toward the floor. Then abruptly he pulled himself up. "No wait. That's what she thought, the greedy bitch. But she was wrong. Look back at ninety-four point five: *does not apply to legal holiday.* The wedding was Labor Day!"

I shook my head, "No, Stone. The wedding would have been Labor Day if Olivia and Oren hadn't squabbled and put it off. By the time they got around to marrying it was well after midnight. Late enough to be Tuesday. Late enough to bar you from the senate. She blackmailed you, and regardless of who pushed whom, she killed you."

"All is forgiven, Mr. Girard. Do you accept that?" the Sub-Authority repeated.

Stone hesitated, his face tightening as I'd seen it over the jade plant. Then he surprised me; he nodded.

As he walked through the double doors at the far side of the courtroom I realized how much he had given up losing his senate seat. The man was meant to be a politician; he knew how to accommodate himself. Now he had accommodated himself into heaven.

I walked back into the hall. The vague scent of brimstone had returned. I had succeeded at this job. The Sub-Authority wouldn't be able to commit me to brimstone. Not yet. But he'd never trust me down below again, either.

I had merely extended my stay on the corridor. If I succeeded case after case I could stay here forever, endlessly ignorant of who I was and why I kept myself here. What had been so horrendous, appalling, galling about my own death to make me less willing to forgive than Stone Girard?

I, the celestial detective, had not a clue.

My left wing felt stiff, tense, tired. I pulled out the book I'd hidden under it. *The Perfect Crime.* Stone Girard's death had hardly been a perfect crime.

I looked at the book and smiled.

The perfect crime had to be mine. So perfect I couldn't part with it. But what crime? Victim or killer? How had I—I peered down toward the book but it was gone.

A new Cool shuffled out of the Hearing Room, head down, face pinched in confusion. Up here the authorities have to be fair. They can't offer one Cool benefits and deny them to the next. I moved beside him. "Need a detective?"

A Contest Fit for a Queen

You can always sunbathe in Berkeley on Washington's Birthday, they say. Maybe so. But it was already Valentine's Day and it had been raining since New Year's. I was willing to believe we'd be able to bathe in another week, but odds were it'd be with a cake of *Ivory*.

Tonight, the thermometer was not ten degrees above freezing (polar by our standards). The rain pounded on the portal like a door-to-door salesman. It was a night made for staying home.

Or it would have been if one of the other tenants in Howard's house hadn't booked the living room for his club meeting. A meeting of the South Campus Respect for Reptiles Committee.

"Do they bring the esteemed with them, Howard?"

"Don't ask. But if you're going through the living room keep your shoes on." Howard shook his head. Clearly, this was a topic he didn't dare dip into. The corners of his mouth twitched. He wanted to dip. His mouth opened and shut again. He was dying to dip.

I grinned.

He gave up. "It's an emergency meeting for the Reptilians, Jill. Their status in the animal rights union has been challenged. By the Save the Goldfish Committee."

35

It took me a moment to recall just what it was snakes ate. "May the better vertebrate win." And thinking of the fish, I added, "I suppose it's too late to make a dinner reservation."

But even before I finished the sentence, I knew the answer. You'll never starve in Berkeley. Even on Valentine's Day there is always a restaurant with an empty table for two. But while Howard insists I am his number one love, number two (this house in which he dwells as Chief tenant and lusts to own) is close behind, and he would never abandon its nurturing nooks and cave-like crannies to the Reptilians.

"Better than that!" he said, running his hand around my back, under my arm till his fingers caressed the side of my breast. "I've got an evening so romantic, a night so exotic, so continental it should have subtitles. The lover's answer," he said pulling me closer, "to one stop shopping."

"Ah-ha. Dinner in bed, you mean."

"And with a new tradition I think you're going to like."

The California King-sized bed was covered with a spotted Madras spread (we'd done dinners here before), and dotted with white cardboard cartons (Styrofoam is outlawed in Berkeley), and plastic plates from freezer dinners. Howard had bought the bed for its mission style headboard with the four-inch wide runner at the top—the perfect size for coffee mugs and wine glasses. (By now we had a number of spotted pillowcases.)

"Happy Valentine's Day," Howard said uncorking the chardonnay. (White goes better with the pillowcases.)

"And to you," I said, saluting him with a spring roll.

From downstairs came a muffled shout. I bit into the spring roll.

He said, "Valentine's Day is a traditional sort of holiday—"

"I thought it had been created by the card companies—"

"So I propose a tradition of our own. A tradition suitable for two esteemed police detectives, like us."

"Here on the bed?"

He leaned forward, puckered his lips, opened his mouth, sucked in the rest of my spring roll. When he'd swallowed, he said, "Valentine's Day collars. Other traditions come later. What's your most memorable Valentine's collar?"

I laughed. Only Howard would come up with a tradition celebrating the best Valentine's Day arrests. I could have negotiated a prize, but as everyone in coupledom knows, no object is to be as cherished as the hard-won right to lord it over one's mate. The Collar Queen, I liked the prospect of that. "In Homicide or patrol?"

"Either one. In your entire time on the force." Howard reached for another spring roll.

I could see the lay of the land here. "Oh no! You first."

"Don't you have a collar?"

"Yeah, I've got one, from when I was on patrol. But I'm no fool, Howard, and if I let you sit and listen for twenty minutes, by the time I finish talking there won't be any food left. You start."

From downstairs came a loud hiss. I preferred to think of it as a delegate's indication of dissent. As opposed to his subject's hiss of disgruntlement.

Rain splatted against the window and the wind scraped the glass with a branch of the jacaranda tree. But in here, enclosed by the warm green walls and the crisp white moldings, with the smells of Asian spices mingling with the aroma of wine, the whir of the space heater, it was turning out to be an okay Valentine's. Howard shepherded half the rice onto his plate, added a heaping scoop of vegetable satay, four chicken brochettes, and a wad of eggplant with black beans. He crossed his long legs, propped his plate on one knee and began. "This is from patrol, too. I'd already been working detective detail but I'd rotated back onto patrol for a while. The call was on a natural death of an LOL. The LOL was in her seventies, but she looked to have been old for that age, not one of the Gray Panthers who'd stomp a mugger into the ground and walk off shaking the dust from her Birkenstocks; no, she was an LOL."

I nodded, leaning against the headboard, balancing my satay on my thigh as I reached for my wine glass.

"She lived in a four-room cottage, west of San Pablo. Hurricane fencing around the perimeter, big dog in the yard. House a square, four identical-size rooms."

"Like a sandwich you cut into quarters?"

"Right. Neighbors heard the dog barking and got concerned that he hadn't been out in that yard all day. Valentine, that was the dog's name, because he had a white heart on his rump."

I smiled. That bit of whimsy made me like the old lady. I could tell it grabbed Howard, too. "How did she die?"

"Heart attack, I think. Certainly, natural cause. And fast, I think. The TV was still on. She was sitting in front of it on one of those maroon flowered antique sofas with the buttons covered in the same material, and all of it looking too hard to sit on. Makes you understand the energy of the Victorian age."

"Had to keep moving, huh?"

"Oh no!" One of the Reptilians shouted downstairs. I glanced at the foot of the door. There wasn't a quarter of an inch between it and the jamb.

Picking up his pace and volume, Howard said, "Not much in her living room—the sofa, one chair, two end tables, a bookcase, a couple pictures on the wall, but no photos or knickknacks strewn around like you find with most LOL's."

"Maybe she didn't have anyone."

"No relatives, right. Nothing unnecessary in the kitchen or the bedroom. Looked like she lived frugally, but not desperately so like a lot of people on social security. She was tidy, and she knew what she liked, that Victorian stuff. If someone had told me it was *eighteen* ninety-four instead of nineteen ninety-four in her house, there wouldn't have been much to contradict it. Even her books tended to be things like Jane Austen."

I finished my satay and glanced at the carton. Despite his monologue, Howard had managed to down his portion and was eyeing the same carton. I served. "So that's it? *That's* your most interesting case?"

"Wait. I haven't gotten to the interesting part: the fourth room. You've got these three austere, Victorian-lady rooms, then the fourth. It was crammed, floor to ceiling, with the oddest collection of stuff I've come across. Golf clubs, electric trains, stamp collection, a set of something like twenty-seven drill bits, leather suitcases, a black plastic stool in which the middle of the cushion comes out, the scroungiest looking stuffed pheasant—thing was missing an eye and all its tail feathers—with a Valentine's heart on a ribbon around its neck."

"Must have been easy to shoot."

Ignoring that, Howard went on. "Place was so full you couldn't even see the windows."

"Her late husband's things?"

"Nope, maiden lady. Neighbors said they'd never seen a male visitor. Besides, some of the stuff was almost new, a lot never used. It wasn't like mementos from the love of her life who died in nineteen forty-nine or fifty-two."

I put down my second spring roll. "It's all guy stuff, except the stool and that's just weird. Things like the drill bits; you'll find women who've got them, but—"

"Yeah, you can picture the owner: one of those guys who *thinks* he's going to be a handyman and his wife or kids give him the complete deluxe home handyman's set. And in this case I'd bet my last spring roll those bits had never been out of the box."

"Over by the door," a Reptilian shouted downstairs.

Howard tensed, ready to charge downstairs and defend his second love from invasion.

I put a hand on his arm. "Berkeley, the city of diversity, should create a snake run, like the dog park. It'd only take a narrow piece of land. Owners'd put their cobras and pythons on little alligator leashes to exercise them. And the best part for the sedentary snake lover, is they wouldn't even have to be in good shape for the walk. Not like our burglar who had to hoist a massage chair, a backbend bench the size of a sofa, and enough photography equipment to furnish a studio."

"Jill, how'd you—"

I put up a hand to quiet him. The thought was tiptoeing across the back of my head, just out of reach. Something about his story . . . somethi—"The fucking pheasant!"

"What?"

"That's what his wife called it." I put down my glass. "Howard, I remember that pheasant. I took the call on the burglary it came from. On Linden Terrace. It was just an ordinary case; I wouldn't remember it at all—it must have been six or seven years ago—but the guy insisted on describing his missing pheasant. Seems it was the first thing he ever shot, and in honor of that he gave it to his wife for Valentine's Day back when they were engaged."

"She married him anyway, huh?" He dumped the satay on his rice.

"For better or worse. He even showed me a picture of it, with the red ribbon and the heart. A velvet heart with lace around it like you'd find on a box of candy."

"Probably where it came from. Guy probably gobbled the chocolates while he was waiting for the pheasant to fly." For Howard, the department's sting king, an uneven match like rifle versus wing is certainly not sport.

It had been years since that burglary. "I suppose there was no reason to confiscate pheasant and company from the old lady's house."

"Hardly. It'd've filled half the evidence room. But the pheasant, I think the neighbor took it, strange as it is to think there could be two human beings who'd want it." Howard fingered the last spring roll and grinned. "So my LOL, Rosamin Minton, was an LOF."

"Little Old Fence?"

"A fence with the worst taste in town. Or a fence who'd moved the electronics and jewelry but couldn't get rid of the rest of the junk." Howard took a bite of satay and nodded. "Still, not a bad Valentine's entry. Not so easy to top. So, Jill, what's your Valentine collar?"

I took a swallow of wine, leaned back against the headboard, adjusted the pillow—that little ledge is great for cups and glasses, but it does nothing for my neck. I picked up my wine glass, looked Howard in the eye and grinned back at him. "You could have won by a mile, Howard. But not now. Your entry was good, a real competitive racer of a case. I was in bad shape . . . until . . . you reminded me." I lifted my wine glass in salute. I don't often win these contests with Howard—nobody does—but when I do I make the most of it. The robes of the Collar Queen were going to hang quite nicely off my shoulders. "The pheasant burglary took place, Howard, on Valentine's Day!"

Howard gave me a tentative salute. He could see he was being edged out, but he wasn't throwing in the towel yet.

"Howard, the RP, what was his name?—I remember thinking it was a funny name for a reporting party—Robert Parton, that's it—he was just outraged that his bird—"

"Flew the coop on Valentine's?"

"Right. His wife did point out that it was on the mantel where he put it for the occasion. A thief could hardly miss it. Then Parton complained about the loss of a stained glass lamp he'd made himself—"

"Lamp with a band of chartreuse hearts at the edge of the shade?"

"Could there be two?" I grinned wider. The lamp had propelled me to neck-and-neck with Howard. "And Parton was really pissed that the thief had used a couple of his old jackets to wrap the things in. His wife kept reminding him that the stereo and the TV were still there and they were worth plenty more than a bag of used clothes, a lamp, and a moldy bird. But Parton wasn't buying that. He ranted at her, at me, and even at the Chihuahua, for God's sake. Like it should have stood off the thief, single paw-edly!"

"That's it? Your whole Valentine offering? You lose! The answer's obvious. The wife did it?"

"*Au contraire,* my dear Howard. Mrs. Parton was out with the doctor at the time of the burglary. And she's hardly the type to hire a few unemployed mafiosi. And more to the point, there were two other burglaries that Valentine's night. And the next year another three with the same MO. And three the following year, when we were half-expecting them and still couldn't prevent them. Drove us crazy. And then they stopped."

"And never started again?" He meant did the thief get pulled in for something else, or merely move out of town?

"Nope, nothing more. Burglary Detail was keeping an eye out. Simpson there really went over those cases, but he couldn't find a link. The Bensquis were in their twenties, the Partons near forty, the Yamamotos in their late sixties. Victims were a bakery chef, an engineer, three artists, one nurse, one doctor, an airline pilot, a copy editor, a short haul-truck driver. There was no connection through their jobs, religious groups, hobbies, clubs—zilch. They were all in different parts of the city. Some victims had standing Valentine's plans, some went out to dinner on the spur of the moment, one couple just went out for a walk, and bingo! Their darkroom was cleaned out! No prints, no suspicious characters, no vans or trucks loitering out front. Stuff never turned up in pawnshops, flea markets, or any of the normal places. Not lead one. And Parton, the doctor . . . well, if he made that number of follow-up calls to any patient, they'd die of shock." I leaned back, took a long swallow of wine and said, "It was a very frustrating case—nine disparate couples, burgled of stuff of no particular value, and it all ends up with one little old lady who kept it sealed away from her in a back room! But, Howard, reward comes to the worthy. And thanks to your accidental discovery, you have given me an assist to winning the First Annual Valentine's Day Collar Contest. Pay homage to the Collar Queen!"

"No you don't! This is a *collar* contest. There was no collar in your case. You, Jill, got nada!"

"Outside! Look outside!" Downstairs doors banged. Howard hesitated, clearly torn between defending his house or his contest.

"It sounds good," I said. "But I'm not using the bathroom till you make sure everyone's accounted for."

Howard headed downstairs and I cleared off the bed the remnants of the first course, preparatory to the more traditional Valentine's Day tradition.

Tomorrow, I'd track down the department's files on the

burglaries. No way was Howard going to win!

What I did not track down the next morning—Monday—was Simpson of Burglary Detail. While Howard and I had been setting our bet, Simpson had been flying off to the Bahamas.

What was waiting for me in the station was a batch of in-custodys held over the weekend. When you bungle your burgling Friday night, the city gives you free lodging all weekend. By Monday morning you are a sorry, and surly, soul. I didn't finish running the checks on the in-custodys before Detective's Morning Meeting, and afterwards ended up transporting one of the surly and sorry to San Mateo County an hour away. In the afternoon I had a court appearance on an old 217 (assault with intent to murder) and I didn't get around to the late Rosamin Minton's neighbor till after 5 o'clock.

The Minton house was just as Howard described it: a square clapboard box behind a hurricane fence, in a neighborhood where shabby didn't stand out. Two scraggly trees now stood watch over the walkway, obviously the work of a newer, if not more horticulturally talented tenant. The present neighbor, the nephew of the pheasant-taker, hadn't known Rosamin Minton. He handed over the contraband bird without question. If he could have asked for a sworn statement that I'd tell no one it had nested in his house, he would have. Clearly, he was too embarrassed to ask why, after all these years, it was needed by the officialdom of his city.

I picked up the thing gingerly. Taxidermy, apparently, is not forever. The bird was not just eyeless and sans tail feathers, there were bare spots on its back, and it looked like it had used one wing to fight off its assailant. Even the lace and velvet heart looked like it had been slobbered over.

★ ★ ★ ★ ★

Robert Parton stared at the deceased bird with an expression of horror that matched my own. "It's been chewed! How could anyone—"

"No accounting for taste, Mr. Parton."

He brushed its moldy feathers. "Still, you found it! After all these years! Monica, it's still got the heart I got for you."

Monica Parton looked even more appalled. A woman of some discretion, I felt.

Only the Chihuahua found merit in the miserable memento. He was running from one side of the spacious living room to the other, bouncing and lowing like he'd treed the foul himself.

"Where did you find it?" Parton asked.

"The other side of Berkeley."

"Did you get my lamp? Stained glass; took me six months to make. And my jackets?"

"Robert," Monica said, "the Salvation Army wouldn't even want those clothes. Be glad you've got your bird."

Before they could continue the sartorial debate, I opened my pad and read off a list of the other Valentine's Day victims. "Do you recognize any of these names?"

"No," Robert said, still holding the pheasant overhead, away from his other admirer.

"Mrs. Parton?"

She looked thoughtful, as if giving the list more consideration than had her booty-enthralled husband. But in the end she shook her head.

"Dr. Parton, I know how concerned you were about this burglary. In the five years since then have you come across anything connected to it? Any motive?"

Both shook their heads. And as I left he was beaming at the bird and she was still shaking her head.

★ ★ ★ ★ ★

It was the next day before I had time to go over the old Valentine burglary files thoroughly enough to make a list of the losses. The stool with the hole belonged to Jason Peabody.

The Peabody house was one of those two-bedroom stucco jobs with one room over the garage. I'd been in enough of them to know that the living room would be too small for an eight-by-ten rug. The whole Peabody house could have fitted in the Parton's living room. It was just before noon when I rang the Peabody bell. And a minute or two after when the door opened.

"Mrs. Peabody? I'm Detective Smith." I held out my shield.

"Yes?" She had that you've-found-me-out look we see so often that we mistake it for a greeting. "Sorry it took me so long. I needed to put Spot in the back room. Come on in."

A leather couch, matching overstuffed chair, and a coffee table made for a normal-sized room pretty much filled the space. The television sat atop the built-in bookcase, blocking the window. The dining room, too, was a space that could not accommodate one more fork or candlestick, much less a chair. I almost felt guilty as I said, "I have good news. We've found the black plastic stool that was taken in your burglary, the one with the cushion that pulls out to create a hole in the middle."

"Jason's toilet seat chair." If she was pleased she was hiding it well.

"Your husband is incapacitated?"

She laughed uncomfortably. "No. No. When you take the center out, the chair looks like a toilet seat, a padded black plastic toilet seat."

"But it's not?"

"Oh, no. I should make you guess what it's for." She almost smiled before she recalled who she was speaking to. I've seen that reaction often enough, too. "Jason kept the stool right there." She pointed to the side of the fireplace, next to the bookcase with the television on it.

The stool was eighteen inches square. With it in place, the Peabodys would have had to inch between it and the coffee table. "What is it?"

"A headstand stool."

Even in Berkeley . . .

"You know, for people who want to do headstands, but don't want all their weight on their heads." She was eyeing my reaction, almost smiling. "They stick their heads through the hole, like they're ready to flush them." She swallowed a laugh. "Then they hang onto the legs and kick up. Jason's tall and thin. He always looked kind of like a fern in the wind with his feet waving back and forth by the mantel as he tried to keep his balance." Now she was laughing. "And the TV; it's a miracle it survived."

On duty, we are not encouraged to join in an RP's merriment, lest they later forget, or regret theirs and become outraged about ours. With some difficulty, I waited for her to stop and said, "One of the other items you lost was a backbend bench."

She glanced at the tiny room. "Oh, jeez, you didn't find that, too, did you?"

I was going to give her the standard "Not yet, but we're still looking" but clearly that was not what she wanted to hear. "No."

She brightened. "Nor the massage chair, or the statue of Shiva?"

"Not yet." I would have noticed a leather recliner and a three-foot tall image of an Indian god of destruction.

"Well, officer, thanks for all your effort. Who would have

thought you'd still be working this case after all these years. We appreciate it. But we'll certainly understand if Jason's stuff doesn't turn up. To tell you the truth, he's gone on to other interests. I doubt he'd attempt a headstand now, even if he had the stool."

"And you'd be hard pressed to make room for the massage chair, or even the Shiva."

It was a moment before she smiled, shrugged and agreed. But that moment said it all.

The next three victims, or wives of the bereft of golf clubs, ratty chairs, garden equipment, books of stamps barely used, aged racing bicycles, aged skis, enough exercise equipment to fill the YMCA, had clearly been warned. Their performances were not worthy of Berkeley Rep., but they'd have made the cut in many little theaters. They were delighted at our discovery, they assured me. Their husbands would be thrilled. They thanked me, thanked the burglary detail, the Berkeley Police Department, and the entire Berkeley criminal community that hadn't gotten around to fencing their conjugal wares.

I didn't believe a word of it.

Esme Olsen, a sturdy gray-haired woman nearer to seventy than sixty, looked as if my knock had jerked her out of another dimension. I found her in her basement folding gold foil carefully along the edges of a piece of teal glass cut in the shape of a tulip leaf. The sketch of the stained glass panel she was working on was pinned to the wall above the glasscutter and extra foil rolls at the far end of the workbench. Irregularly shaped pieces of glass—red, yellow, green, and three shades of purple—filled the rest of the bench and larger sheets stood in specially made cases behind her. On the top of the cabinet was a photo—probably fifteen years old—of her and a white-haired man as happy-go-lucky as she was intense.

It was almost a formality when I asked, "How would you feel if I told you we're on the trail of your husband's tools: the drill bits, the straight saw, the jig saw, the shag-toothed saws, the clamps, the hammers and all?"

"Oh, my God! You're not bringing that junk back here?" No Berkeley Rep. role for her! And from the horror that lined her face as she looked around her stained glass studio, I could picture the room in its previous incarnation.

"Your husband didn't do much work in this shop, did he?" It was a hunch, but a solid one.

"Work? No. Oh, he had intentions. He'd get on a kick about building bookcases. At one time we had six of them upstairs, more cases than books, I told him. Fortunately they came apart before he could find things to fill them with. Then he thought he'd build a gazebo. He had wood stacked in the yard for a year, and kindling enough down here to cook the entire house. Then there was the hope chest, or more accurately hope*less* chest. For a while he bought used tables and chairs and thought he was going to refinish them. See, he liked the *idea* of woodworking better than the precision of it."

Some police officers never get suspects so naively open with the police. But I've dealt with enough artists in Berkeley to know that the shift from their total absorption in the visual takes a while, and as they cross the bridge from right brain to left brain good sense can stumble over the railing. "So you gave yourself a Valentine's Day gift. You arranged for his stuff to be 'stolen.' "

She didn't answer. She'd zoomed to the other end of the bridge. And what she found there horrified her. I wouldn't have been surprised if this was the first time it truly struck her that she'd committed a crime.

The eight co-conspirators had warned each other; why hadn't they told Esme Olsen? It made me a whole lot less sympathetic to them. I wanted to reassure Esme Olsen, but I couldn't do that until she answered the questions everyone who'd worked the case had. How did the nine conspirators know each other? We'd been over every possible connection between them. Where did they come meet to conspire? Did they get together for afternoon tea and complaints, or drive to bars to map out their burglaries? And Rosamin Minton, how did she come to have the loot stashed at her house? "The police department takes a very dim view of false reporting."

She took a step back and actually looked even smaller than she was. "I didn't mean to get the police involved, honestly, Officer. I thought Harry would have left dealing with the police to me. I thought I'd just *tell* him I reported his stuff missing."

"Give me the names of the other women you planned this with."

She took another step back.

"Ms. Olsen, you have broken the law. The police department has spent tens of hours investigating. We've had patrol officers, sergeants, and inspectors on this case. This is a serious matter. The names . . . ?"

She looked tinier, paler, older than at any moment since I arrived. In a small voice, she said, "I don't know."

"You planned an elaborate heist that took place over several years, Valentine's Day after Valentine's Day, and you're telling me you don't know the names of your co-conspirators?"

"Yes." For an instant I thought she was going to explain that. Then she shut her mouth tight, like a little kid who'd rather be sent to her room than rat on her friends.

Friends who didn't deserve her sacrifice. "I'm afraid I'm

going to have to take you to the station."

Her face scrunched in panic, but her question was not what I would have expected. "How long will that take?"

"Till your lawyer bails you out, Mrs. Olsen."

Her face fell. She really did look horrified. I wondered how long she had been hidden away down here away from the realities of society.

"I've got to be back by quarter to four," she insisted plaintively. "I've got an appointment at the vet at four."

I'd seen everything from Airedales to Chihuahuas today. I realized now that this was the first house I'd visited where if I hadn't been greeted by a dog. I hadn't even heard one barking in a back room. "I didn't see a dog?"

"When he's healthy he'd greet you at the gate. He's sick. On antibiotics. I'm keeping him in the back room. Oh, the vet says he'll be fine; and I believe him. I'm probably worrying for nothing, but my old dog died suddenly two years ago and I just don't want to take any chances now."

Now it all fell into place. I loved the idea of nine average Berkeley women who'd taken their spousal clutter into their own hands. A little service for each other. Personalized burglaries—we go to the address provided and steal only what you don't want. No wonder the televisions and compact disks, computers and the diamond rings had been untouched while the wily 'thieves' made off with aged hacksaws and headstand stools. Now I realized why her friends hadn't warned her. They hadn't seen her today. I smiled. "You weren't lying about not knowing their last names, were you?"

"Oh no. I wouldn't lie to the police."

"You all met at the dog run, right? And your dog was too sick to go out today."

She nodded.

"You could tell me the name of every one of their dogs,

right, but you don't know their owner's names?" I knew enough about dog walking to understand that phenomena. By now, after years in the conspiracy, Esme Olsen might be able to call the humans by first name, but she wouldn't have a clue about last names. "You can skip the women, just tell me what the dogs were called."

She looked puzzled, but so relieved she didn't question my demand. "Let me see, Lucy is the black lab, and Sacha's the poodle. Then there's Emmet, the yellow lab pup, and Emily—she's mostly Tibetan terrier—and Hannah, the basset, and Sierra—he's a Chihuahua, and—wait a minute—oh, yes, MacTavish, the Scotty."

"And Val is your dog?"

She smiled before she realized she'd exposed her connection to Rosamin Minton.

Then she took me upstairs to see the whiskered brown mongrel with the white heart on his rump. He was a dog definitely on the mend.

"You went to a lot of trouble planning the burglaries. Why didn't you give the stuff to the Salvation Army?"

"Couldn't. That's where Harry shopped for the furniture to refinish. We never thought we'd be endangering Rosamin. She swore she didn't need that extra room. And she *did* need the twenty dollars a month we each gave her. And, Officer, it really did comfort her to know one of us would take Val when she died."

I smiled at her. We were still in the shadow of Valentine's Day, when acts of love are expected. And, I had to admit, there were a few items of Howard's for which I'd have hired Esme and Colleagues. For his tenant's snake I'd have given them a bonus. Besides, the city wouldn't want to look ridiculous in court.

There'd be some paperwork and formalities with this case

later. And after that, I'd accept Howard's concession in the First Annual Collar Contest. But for now, I scratched Val gently behind one floppy ear, said, "Okay, Val, I'll leave you your mistress. Consider this your Valentine's gift," and smiled magnanimously.

Because, after all, magnanimity is a fitting quality for a Queen.

Karma

Chapter 1

"That's the Mani Lakhang over there, Jill." Ginny Daly pointed to a rectangular, one-story, stucco-and-shingle building.

"The Mani Lakhang?" Even in the Telegraph Avenue area of Berkeley, where once stately Victorians had been carved into apartments for students of the nearby University of California—where the antiwar demonstrations and drugs of the sixties had given way to the cults and drugs of the seventies—this building stood out for its neglect. Inspired by the rising value of real estate, owners of surrounding houses had begun refurbishing. But on a corner lot large enough for three of those houses, the Mani Lakhang slumped behind a high stucco wall and a yellowed lawn of weeds.

"Temple. In Bhutanese that means temple."

"Oh." I pulled the car over and began backing into a parking spot. According to Ginny, the temple was occupied by a Buddhist holy man from Bhutan, a man named Padmasvana. Bhutan was a small Himalayan country located between India and Tibet. Already it was more than I wanted to know.

When I'd called Ginny, I'd had in mind going out for a movie or a drink, certainly not attending a blessing ceremony by a Bhutanese lama.

But I had to make an effort. I had to get out, renew friendships, do new things. I wasn't married anymore. When I had been married I hadn't thought that marriage or my husband, Nat, took much of my time. But now that we were separated I found that his presence—or the promise of it and, finally, the threat of it—had influenced my hours much more than I cared to admit.

I shut off the car's engine and stared at the temple, trying to recall what I had heard about it. "There was an overdose here," I said slowly. "A year ago August, when I was on vacation. Some boy died of an overdose."

Ginny sighed.

"And they do something in the morning that gives off a lot of smoke. The neighbors complained."

"Honest to God, Jill, you've been a cop too long. Even when you're off duty, you sound like a cop."

"Nat used to say that."

"Well, he was right." Ginny opened the car door and stepped out. "Are you coming?"

"Uh-huh." I locked the car and together we walked across the street to the temple. Some officers avoided their beats when they were off duty, but I liked the area around Telegraph Avenue, with its sidewalk craftsmen, its funky shops, the University Museum and the coffee houses. For me, avoiding Telegraph would have meant doing without a big part of Berkeley.

Inside the temple—after we had given our donations to a red-robed boy at the door—the first thing that struck me was the pungent smell of incense. The smoke drifted from burners along the walls and on the altar, and formed a haze beneath the ceiling.

At a glance the room looked like any makeshift church, with a stage at the front and a center aisle dividing two rows of wooden folding chairs. But there the simplicity stopped. The room was ablaze with color. Crimson walls were crowded with larger-than-life pictures of Oriental holy men. On small altars beneath the pictures were brass bowls filled with shiny red apples, crystal vases holding white carnations and the ubiquitous incense burners. As they pushed toward their seats, a number of people paused to bow before the pictures.

Ginny hurried me along down the center aisle and into an empty seat. "We're lucky to get such good seats. I mean, a lot of times they have to turn people away."

"Mmm."

The stage was about ten rows in front of us. Around the periphery of the stage was a foot-high lattice. The altar, slightly right of center stage as we looked at it, was draped in a brocade of gold, electric blue and orange. On either side of the altar were six spinning, four-foot-high cloth cylinders— rather like huge gaudy lamp shades.

Behind the altar was a giant picture of a young Oriental— Padmasvana, presumably. His face was rectangular, his cheekbones high; his eyes, large and dark, caught the light in a way that gave the impression he was looking directly at me.

It was his smile, though, that stood out. All the lines around his mouth seemed relaxed, as if this were his normal expression. And behind that smile lurked an invitation to join his happiness.

I was surprised at how much the man's picture affected me.

I looked away, turning my attention to the rest of the stage. On either side of the altar was a chair upholstered in satin brocade. And in a row at the rear of the stage were more of those gaudy cloth cylinders.

"What are those?" I pointed.

Ginny smiled. It was a smile that seemed to cover a

growing irritation. "Prayer wheels," she said.

"Prayer wheels?"

"Prayer wheels are found all through the Himalayas. You spin them to send off a prayer."

At the moment, however, the wheels were not being spun manually. A forced-air duct at one side of the stage was responsible for their continuing supplications.

In the few minutes since we had arrived the room had almost filled. The audience was a cross section of Berkeley: the usual assortment of people in embroidered shirts and jeans, older women in muslin blouses, younger ones in leather skirts, men in cords, men in suits and rumpled teenage boys who looked as though they had walked nonstop from Bhutan. And there were the guru's followers— "Penlops," Ginny called them. They stood wearily at the door, their hands tucked in the pouches of their coarse red monk's robes.

The crash of a gong reverberated through the room. The house lights went off, leaving only the stage illuminated.

A middle-aged, rather portly Caucasian man strode to center stage. His white silk shirt and slacks fit snugly. Against the cacophonous colors behind him, he stood out like a plump cloud.

The stage lights dimmed. A spotlight surrounded him.

"Welcome. Welcome." His deep voice cut through the rumbles of conversation. "I am Rexford Braga. Some of you already know me."

From the audience rose hesitant laughter at this show of modesty.

Braga smiled. "I want to thank you for coming and to assure you that the blessing Padmasvana will bestow on you will enrich your karma in this incarnation and in future incarnations."

"What's his connection with all this?" I whispered.

"Shh. He brought Padma to this country."

I wanted to ask Ginny more, but she was pointedly ignoring me to focus on Braga, so I settled back to watch. Standing before the altar, rocking slightly on his heels, Braga began recounting his contacts with the guru: how they had sparked his potential, how he had become more attuned to his inner consciousness—less involved with the material world. "That is why Padmasvana came halfway around the world to live with us. And to give us all his blessing."

A murmur of approval went up.

"This is a great compliment to you."

The murmur was louder.

"It is the higher consciousness that you here in Berkeley, and in the San Francisco Bay area, have shown that brought Padmasvana."

Applause.

"It is for *you* that he established his temple here."

More applause.

"Because *you* had the wisdom, the insight, to come here, *you* showed yourselves to be worthy of his blessing."

More applause.

"This is a great tribute to *you*."

Cheers.

"Tonight you will grow. You will expand your consciousness. You will realize!"

The cheers were wild. I looked at Ginny. She was clapping and yelling, her face alight.

Perhaps Braga was right. I had already realized something, though perhaps not what Braga intended. I had realized that there were worse things than spending an evening alone. But still, I had to admit an interest in seeing the guru.

It was several minutes before the cheers subsided. Braga

made a few procedural comments and departed, to more cheers.

The incense grew thicker. The audience became silent in expectation. The stage lights became brighter.

Padmasvana—recognizable from his picture—appeared. He was tall for an Oriental, dressed in a loose gold robe that hung open from his shoulders. Underneath it he wore what appeared to be a thin T-shirt and pants, also gold. Around his waist was a crimson sash. Behind him came another man: shorter, older, but very similar in dress, coloring and features.

Padmasvana bowed to the audience. He smiled, the same warm, personal smile as in the picture. Then he bent over the lattice at the edge of the stage to clasp the upstretched hands of the people in the first row, holding each hand between his own for a few seconds.

"It's like he's touched us all," Ginny whispered. As the guru moved back to center stage, the whir of the forced air was louder, the prayer wheels spun faster. The room seemed warmer, the incense heavier. He bowed to the audience and sat in the chair to the right of the altar. The other man sat in the remaining chair.

The stage lights dimmed, leaving only two spotlights on the men.

The guru said something in what I assumed to be Bhutanese.

"Who's he, Ginny?" I asked, indicating the shorter man.

"Chupa-da. He's Padma's assistant."

". . . welcomes you to the Ceremony of Dissolution of Hate," Chupa-da said, pronouncing each syllable carefully in an accent more guttural than Chinese but with the same sing-song rhythm.

The guru spoke again. In spite of my skepticism I felt drawn to the man.

"The blessing you receive," the assistant translated, "is handed down through twenty-two incarnations. Padmasvana is the twenty-second incarnation. The blessing will take hate from your life. Hate will be no longer." He stopped and the younger man spoke again.

"When hate is gone," the assistant went on, "you are free from a shackle. You have the freedom to live. You move higher." He looked toward the guru as if expecting him to continue.

Padmasvana stared silently at the audience, his expression now one of sadness. The sudden disappearance of his usual warmth must have shocked the audience, for uneasy murmurs came from all parts of the room.

The guru spoke, but his words were too soft to make out.

The assistant jerked toward him.

The guru sat forward. He said, "I will go."

A gasp filled the room.

"I thought he didn't speak English," I whispered.

"Not till two weeks ago."

"Soon," Padmasvana said, "I will go."

Cries of *"No!"* rose from the audience. From the front row a gray-haired woman in the red robe of a Penlop jumped up sobbing.

The guru put out his hands for silence. Immediately all human sounds ceased. Only the whir of forced air was audible. Looking at the audience, he spoke slowly. "I carry the guilt of the young Penlop. I . . ."

The assistant jumped up from his chair into the dimly lit space beyond the spotlights. He circled behind his master, then moved in front of him, bowing and nodding.

Padmasvana stood up and adjusted his shoulders in a movement that, had he been a Westerner, I would have called a shrug. He bowed to the altar and walked to the far right of the stage, stopping in front of the farthest prayer wheel. He bowed, spun it, moved to the next, bowed and spun it, and so on until all twelve had received his touch.

The room was silent. I glanced at Ginny. Her eyes were wide, her attention riveted. I wanted to cough but swallowed instead.

The guru nodded to his assistant. The assistant bowed, paused and backed from the stage, through a door at the audience's left. His spotlight went out, leaving the stage lighted by the single circle on Padmasvana.

He sat cross-legged before the altar, facing us, and began a monosyllabic chant. Arms raised, he gestured to encourage the audience, and voices throughout the room picked up the sounds. *"Oh da gya chai."* At first they were hesitant, then surer. *"Oh da gya chai."*

The guru chanted louder.

The audience chanted louder.

The guru's volume increased again and the audience followed, again and again, till the room shook with the sounds. *"Oh da gya chai."*

The prayer wheels spun. The incense smoked. I had the sensation of sitting in a warm swirling bath.

The guru uttered one last chant, a roar.

He lowered his hands to his sides.

The room seemed to reverberate with the sudden silence.

The guru uncrossed his legs, turned to the altar, knelt before it, his body flush against the brocade cloth, his arms raised, his face lifted above the edge of the altar.

In the silence, the sound he uttered seemed like a howl.

He continued to kneel motionless for a moment, then half rose and turned to the audience, his eyes open wide.

A knife protruded from his chest.

Chapter 2

All around us in the darkened room people screamed and cried. Ahead of me a woman fainted. I clambered over Ginny, feeling my way to the aisle, and ran toward the light on the stage.

The guru lay on his back moaning softly. Blood seeped from his chest.

I yanked open the two altar cloths, but behind them was only the underside of a table—no one hiding there. To the audience I yelled, "Someone turn on the lights. Is there a doctor here? A doctor? Everyone keep your seats. I'm a police officer. Is there a doctor?"

The lights came on. Through the commotion a woman on the left aisle called out, "I'm a doctor."

"Hurry. Let her through. And you," I said to the nearest red-robed Penlop, "call the police. Tell them what's happened and where. Tell them the beat officer is already here."

Without comment, the boy ran for the door.

I looked down at the guru. His face was taut with panic. Weakly, he clutched at the knife.

His lips moved.

Putting up a hand to silence the crowd, I bent down.

His eyes opened wider.

The doctor knelt on his far side. She touched my arm.

The guru's mouth opened. Ignoring the doctor, I leaned closer. Again his lips moved, but no sound came out.

"Officer," the doctor said, "give me room. This man doesn't have time to waste."

She had not raised her voice, but it was loud enough for the excitable gray-haired woman in the first row. She let out a scream.

All noise stopped.

The silence was broken only by the woman's cries: "My son, oh my son!" She lunged forward, her hands grasping for a hold at the edge of the stage. Her shrieks turned to wordless keenings. She lurched at the stage again, her fingers grabbing at the flower-covered lattice, but there was no hold and she slipped back.

Who was she, this aging woman dressed like a Penlop? That, I'd have to . . .

On the stage the side door banged and Rexford Braga ran toward me, his white shirt stained with perspiration, a cigarette clasped between his fingers. The guru's assistant was right on his heels. Braga stared down at the guru. "What's going—Hey, what's he doing? What the—"

The doctor glared up.

Braga didn't look horrified or sickened or even sorrowful—his expression showed only indignation from the wounded figure toward the gold-robed assistant who stood motionless behind him. Putting his arm around the man's shoulder, Braga tried to draw him away toward the edge of the stage. Chupa-da shook loose, all the time staring down at his stricken leader.

With a parting pat on the unresponsive shoulder, Braga moved to center stage. "Ladies and gentlemen, please give me your attention."

Slowly, the audience quieted.

Pulling my badge from my purse and showing it to Braga before I pinned it on my shirt, I said, "Tell them to stay in their seats."

"Ladies and gentlemen, please remain seated. Please sit down. This has been a horrible experience for us all. Terrible. Terrible." Braga's glance wandered over the audience with none of the personalized intensity that had characterized his previous monologue. Was he, I wondered, more distressed than he appeared? He swallowed. "Padmasvana in his wisdom has a reason for what has happened—so that you should learn a lesson, a very difficult lesson." He moved closer to the audience. "Just as Jesus Christ died on the cross, just as Buddha died, uh, as all great spiritual leaders have—"

Moans rose from the audience.

Braga did a double take. "I didn't say he was dying!" Again he swallowed. "We are not in a position to know what Padma has planned. We cannot know his karma. But we do know he has done this for you. For your benefit . . ."

The ambulance crew burst through the door, followed by the lab crew and six patrol officers. As the beat officer on the scene, this case would be mine.

I had just finished instructing the officers to get the names and addresses and row numbers of those in the audience when the ambulance men slipped the guru onto a stretcher and started down the steps. The guru's assistant started after it, but an officer stopped him.

I looked pointedly at the doctor.

"He won't make it to the hospital," she whispered.

Four officers moved to the last row of the audience and started taking down names and addresses, working their way from the sides to the center aisle until they'd meet and begin on the next row. It would be a long, tedious process.

Again Braga faced the audience and started to speak, but his words died in mid-sentence. The required mood was gone. The crowd was restless, watching the print man as he spread powder near the spot where Padmasvana had fallen, murmuring in reaction to the flash of the photographer's bulbs.

Turning his back to them, Braga paced to the rear. As he neared the wall, the guru's assistant, Chupa-da, grabbed his arm. His words were muffled, but anguish was etched on his round face.

Braga shrugged.

"Miss, Miss." Chupa-da rushed toward me. "I must go. I must be with Padmasvana. He will need me."

Softly, I said, "No, he won't. He's probably already dead."

He stared, unbelieving.

"I'm sorry."

Without comment, he walked back toward the wall. The residue of shock was visible on his face. The stiffness of his walk and the tremor of his hands suggested that only by a great effort of will was he managing to contain his distress.

I looked away, an awful feeling of helplessness welling up inside. Above the altar, Padmasvana's likeness still smiled down.

Forcing myself to be professional, I surveyed the stage itself. The only access to it was through the side door that Braga had used. Steps that led to the audience had been blocked off with giant pictures of deities. The stage was about four feet high and the latticework railing that extended up from its edge added another foot or so. Only a pole-vaulter could have got to Padmasvana from the audience. I caught myself thinking how ridiculous it was even to pursue this line

68

of thought. Padmasvana's presence was so mesmerizing that the audience's attention had been firmly fixed on the stage. No one could have attacked him that way unseen.

Catching the pacing Braga on a turn, I said, "Where were you during the ceremony?"

He stopped. "What?" He glanced at the crowd and, turning back to me, lowered his voice. "I was downstairs in my office taking care of the donations." When I let my gaze rest on him, he added, "I've already been blessed. I am free of hate. You don't need it more than once."

"Smith?" It was the print man addressing me. "The altar's been done," he said. "Everything but the brass box. You want that?"

I turned to the altar. It stood a few feet right of center stage. The brocade cloths had been pulled slightly apart, revealing the edge of a yellow metal folding table that had probably held tea and cookies at P.T.A. meetings. Still on the altar, still sending smoke on high, were four incense burners, and in the middle sat a long, narrow brass box, studded with what appeared to be rubies. The box was the right shape to have held the knife. Its lid was fastened by a snap hinge that would catch on impact. The guru could have pulled the knife from it while shielding it from view with his body. He could have plunged the knife into his chest as the lid of the box snapped back. I didn't know why Padmasvana would kill himself, but motive would wait.

To the print man I said, "Yes." He reached toward it.

"Cease!" Chupa-da yelled.

The room turned silent once more.

"Do not touch the Tsali-deho."

"You mean this box?"

"The Tsali-deho. Only Padmasvana can open the Tsali-deho." He stepped between us and the box, his hands shaking visibly. All the emotion he had been trying so hard to control up to now seemed ready to burst out.

Pausing for a moment to show we were not about to grab for the box, I said, "What is inside the Sally, uh—" I pointed to it.

Chupa-da bowed his head. Clasping his shaking hands together, he said, "The Tsali-deho holds holy incense. Padmasvana frees the incense at the finish of his blessing. It is very holy."

"Is that all that's inside?" A few sticks of incense would hardly fill the box. There would have been plenty of room for the knife. The box was the only place the knife could have been.

"Only incense is inside," Chupa-da said. "Incense is very important. In Bhutan, Padmasvana used it to keep away evil spirits. But here"—he glanced sharply at the audience—"here people do not believe in spirits. People believe only what their eyes see. They think they are as gods. What they choose to believe—only that exists. Here Padmasvana used the holy incense to end his blessing. A symbol, Westerners say. We allow that."

"I understand," I said, choosing my words carefully. I could feel the growing tension in the room. "But I have to see the inside of the box."

"No!"

"It is possible the knife could have been in there."

"No!"

Chupa-da's voice had risen to a shout. The audience gasped. Braga moved away, seeming to shrug off the dispute as unworthy of his attention.

I called him back. I needed his intervention. The last thing I wanted was an international incident, an accusation that a Berkeley police officer had violated a Bhutanese temple.

"Braga," I said, and a note of appeal was in my voice, "I have to check the box. I won't disturb the incense, but I must see it."

Braga looked from me to Chupa-da and back, his face tense. "Look, I, uh—"

"Women cannot touch the Tsali-deho!" Chupa-da yelled.

Distractedly, Braga ran a hand over his hair. He glanced at the audience and back to the box. "It has to be opened," I said.

Braga's hand moved toward it, but he stopped halfway. "Only Padmasvana's most trusted disciple may exercise that duty."

As one, the audience inhaled.

Pointedly, I stared at Braga.

"No, Officer, I can't open it. I am not a disciple. I am an associate." His voice rose as he made the distinction.

Without looking, I knew every eye in the house was on us.

"It has to be opened," I repeated.

To Chupa-da, Braga said, "Naturally I am not as well versed as you are in the laws of Buddhism, though"—his voice grew louder—"I am not ignorant. There are laws that govern normal circumstances in Bhutan, but here in America"—he shifted, facing the audience—"circumstances change. There may be nothing written in the holy books to cover these circumstances, but Padmasvana would have expected you to do what is necessary."

When the smaller man made no move, Braga said, "Padmasvana would have expected it."

The fans hummed, the prayer wheels whirled. The audience held its breath. Chupa-da stood motionless. Then, facing the box, he extended his hand slowly and, with one move, jerked open the lid. As the box clattered to the floor, I jumped back. The audience gasped. Sticks of incense tumbled out and Chupa-da fell to his knees, feverishly gathering them up.

I stared down at him. The box would have to be checked, of course, but from the number of incense sticks that had been crammed inside, no one could have fitted in a knife, too.

Sighing I leaned back against one of the two chairs, ignoring the grumbling from the audience. So the knife had not been hidden in the box. Where had it come from? Chupa-da was dressed as Padmasvana had been—in a flowing robe that hung open over a gold T-shirt and pants. There was no place to conceal a knife. As he stood up, I noted the tight fit of the shirt as it outlined his ribs—a perfect target to drive a knife into.

I tried to run the minute prior to the stabbing through my mind. I remembered Padmasvana kneeling, his arms raised, his chin just above the edge of the altar. He had made no move that could be construed as stabbing.

And yet he had been alone on stage.

His assistant was tucked away downstairs, his followers beyond the barrier of the stage. Did the guru have any enemies? What if he did? Had they flown down invisibly to stab him?

There was only one conclusion that could be drawn from the facts I had—one of the facts had to be wrong. One seemingly solid fact was not as solid as I had thought. As I reviewed the scene once again, it became obvious where the break had to be.

Chapter 3

I borrowed a flashlight from a patrol officer and, pushing back the altar curtain, shone it on the floor. There just might be a trapdoor . . . and there it was.

I beckoned the print man, and while he dusted the trapdoor, the ladder that hung from it and the area below, I briefed Connie Pereira, one of the patrol officers who would assist me. Then, leaving her in charge, I climbed down the ladder, noting the grime-covered nails that secured it at the top.

The basement room I found myself in was the width of the stage. The temple was built on a down slope so that the front door was at ground level, but the rear section—where the stage was—was sufficiently above ground to allow space for this half basement.

Along all four walls were brightly labeled cartons of Padma Herb Tea. The weary red-robed Penlops were a familiar sight, hawking their tea at all hours of the day on Berkeley streets. I wondered how much this little enterprise grossed. From the persistence with which the Penlops tackled prospective customers (and from the number of complaints we'd had), it should have been quite a profitable business.

Four doors led from the room. Up a few steps behind me was a small, low door. I pulled it open and found myself facing the first row of the audience in the temple. I shut it before anyone noticed me.

At the rear of the room was a door to the outside. It was locked.

Still, anyone who had access to the key—or a credit card to loid the lock—could have entered here and popped up through the trapdoor to kill Padmasvana.

Coming back down the steps I looked at the two remaining walls. One was blank; the other held two doors—one at the top of the stairs that led to the side of the stage, the one Braga had used, and a lacquered red door.

I pushed open the red door.

The room behind it might have been a well-appointed law office, with its rosewood desk and padded leather chair, its Oriental rug and, in the far corner, an antique safe. On top of the safe were piles of greenbacks—mostly fives—enough to make theft a very inviting prospect. I crossed the room toward it.

"Hold it!"

I spun to face a handgun and Rexford Braga.

"Oh, it's you," he said, eyeing my jeans. He lowered the weapon and, glancing at it, added, "It's okay. I have a permit."

"Do you always carry a gun, Mr. Braga?"

"Of course not. I keep it here in my desk. You can ask anyone. They all know I keep it in the desk drawer. It's for protection."

"Protection. Were you afraid one of Padmasvana's followers might hold you up?"

He strode past me, planting himself in front of the money-laden safe. Taking a breath, he stood up straighter and looked at me as he might have done with an audience. "Of course, Officer, I have no such worries about the devotees. Certainly none of them would consider theft, even though crime had become a way of life for many before they came under the light of Padmasvana. Some of the devotees were on drugs, many had stolen, but since they have been here at the ashram, they have come to understand the benefits of the spiritual life.

"No, Officer, it is not our devotees I worry about. But surely you, of all people, are aware of the crime rate in Berkeley. Anyone could break in the back door. I do keep the office locked when the donations are here. I make sure everyone knows that. You see, Officer"—he waited till I had nodded—"you see, I realize that precaution is the best protection."

I felt as if he were expecting applause. "So, Mr. Braga, that means anyone could have come through the basement and you wouldn't have noticed. And anyone familiar with your routine could have counted on that."

"Yes, I suppose that's true. It's a very uncomfortable idea, some stranger prowling here."

"Less uncomfortable than the alternative." Braga said nothing but instinctively moved closer to the piles of cash. In the silence I took time to observe him. Up close there was nothing outstanding about the man. He was shorter than average, about thirty pounds overweight—a factor that he had ignored when choosing his shirt. Braga had grown his hair long and sprayed it down; it hung in stiff clumps over his collar. His eyes were pale, his nose a line between the swells of his cheeks, his mustache mirrored the weak curve of his chin. Unquestionably, Braga was someone who looked better from a distance.

"About the receipts, Mr. Braga. How much do you have there?"

"Nearly six hundred. Could have had more. Every seat was filled. Padma was drawing better and better. Particularly tonight, he—" Braga looked away. "I didn't mean—"

"What did you mean, then?"

"Well . . . I suppose . . ."

"What is it?"

"It's just that, well, during the ceremony Padma spoke a few words of English."

"Yes, I know."

"Well, many of the devotees thought that he planned to atone for the evil they had done before they became his followers."

"Are you saying that Padmasvana decided to die tonight? That he stabbed himself?"

Braga shook his head, a small motion that barely agitated the clumps of hair on his collar. "No, no, Officer, I am not saying anything definite. I'm merely telling you that this was a feeling among some of the devotees."

"But stabbing? Wouldn't that be a rather violent way of dying?"

"Perhaps. Padmasvana was a very advanced being. Who are we to question his methods?"

"Why would the devotees think that, Mr. Braga?"

"The words 'I go.' You see, he had said them before, during the last two ceremonies."

"And what do *you* think he meant?"

Braga shrugged. "How can I say? Perhaps the words were merely sounds—his English was very sketchy. English is a very difficult language. It is entirely different from Bhutanese, you see. Learning English was a very ambitious undertaking for Padma."

"Then how did Chupa-da come to speak so fluently? Isn't he from Bhutan, too?"

Braga pushed a clump of hair from his forehead. "Yes, of course, but there was a difference in *dharma*—in vocation, that is. What I mean is that they were trained differently, for different callings. You see, Officer, when a great leader like Padma is born, it is not without warning. Prophecies are given telling when he will be reincarnated and where. When he is born, the spiritual leaders are waiting. He is not left to grow up like other children. He is taken to the monastery, brought up on a diet of Buddhist teachings, taught all the esoteric knowledge that he will need to be a great leader."

Braga paced to the far side of the room and halfway back. "Padmasvana learned only spiritual things. Now, Chupada, Officer, also studied in the monastery, but he was raised to be a scribe. He was destined to be in charge of correspondence with people in India. Bhutan is right next to India. Anything that is shipped in must come from India. India is Bhutan's pipeline to the rest of the world. So, it behooves each monastery to have a few monks trained to deal with the Indians."

"But don't Indians have languages closer to what they speak in Bhutan than English?"

Braga sighed. "Doubtless they do, but there are so many dialects in India, just as there are in Bhutan. Why, do you realize, Officer, that Bhutan, a Himalayan country of less than a million people, has eight major dialects? You can imagine how many there are in India. No one in either country could expect to travel a hundred miles and understand the local tongue. That is why India has made English a state language."

"Mr. Braga, I still don't understand about the 'I go.' I don't—"

A rookie hurried into the office. "Are you Officer Smith?" He eyed my jeans and shirt.

"Yes. I was off duty when I came here."

He nodded. "Pereira sent me. We've finished with the

people in the audience. She wants to know if you need them for anything."

"No. Tell her to let them go. Then round up the boys in the red robes. I'm going to check out the rest of this place. Tell Pereira to finish up upstairs."

"Right."

To Braga I said, "I want to see the rest of the complex."

"The ashram?"

"Is that where Padmasvana lived?"

"Yes. . . . Okay, I'll get Chupa-da to take you there. It'll be better for him to keep occupied."

Braga hurried upstairs, with undisguised relief.

In a moment Chupa-da followed Braga down the steps leading from the side stage door. He had used the time upstairs to pull himself together, and now his hands were under control. He merely looked pale and a bit dazed.

Without comment, he led me out the back door onto the lawn behind the temple. To my right, the grass flashed red, tinted by the lights of the patrol cars. Squeals from the radios mingled with the grumbles of devotees as they emerged in small groups from the temple.

Chupa-da led me across the lawn to a three-story brown-shingle building. It was in the corner of the lot away from either street and about thirty feet behind the temple. From the outside it was just a house, but inside it looked like a maze. Each room, except the kitchen and the dining room, had been broken up into cells approximately four by six feet. The better ones had windows. The rest had bare walls, a sleeping bag, a round pillow that I recognized as a meditation cushion and a small, framed copy of the picture of Padmasvana that hung behind the altar. I wasn't totally familiar with the housing code, but this had to be breaking plenty of regulations.

"How many people live here?" I asked.

"Padmasvana has twenty-four Penlops."

"And they live in these cells?"

Chupa-da turned to me, shaking his head slowly. "We are all in cells. Life is a cell. In Bhutan, we know this. Here in Berkeley people are ignorant. The Westerners, they decorate their 'cells' with music, with large houses, with theaters and parties. They think if they put enough things in them, the cells will not be cells anymore. But Padmasvana teaches the Penlops to see a cell as a cell and to work to get out of it."

"The Penlops seem to have succeeded." All the cells were empty.

Chupa-da headed up the central staircase. "The Penlops do not return—except at mealtimes—until two o'clock on any night," he said. "Their days are totally devoted to Padmasvana."

We turned left from the landing and were aced with more cells. "They put in long days," I said.

"This life is short, and many of the Penlops have bad karma to overcome. Some have been very violent."

We were at the end of the hallway, and I still hadn't seen the guru's room. Looking around for a door that could lead to a large comfortable room of the same ilk as Braga's office, I asked, "Where is Padmasvana's room?"

Chupa-da looked surprised. "Here." He indicated the cell on his left. It was a copy of all the others except that it contained no picture of the guru. Instead, next to the sleeping bag was a pile of books.

I bent down. There were several volumes on Buddhism, plus an English-Bhutanese dictionary.

"Padmasvana was studying English so he could speak directly to his followers," Chupa-da said quickly.

Picking up W. Y. Evans-Wentz's *The Tibetan Book of the*

Dead, I said, "This is a pretty difficult book to be learning from."

"For most people, yes; for Padmasvana, no."

Replacing the book, I glanced through the pile. Underneath the book was a newspaper clipping—"Felcher, Robert V., beloved son of Vernon Felcher and Elizabeth Grace Felcher of Visalia. Memorial services . . ." It was the obituary of the boy who had overdosed in the ashram.

I had heard about the incident when I had returned from vacation more than a year ago. There had been rumors that the ashram was a way station for Mexican drugs. When Bobby Felcher died, the department had turned the ashram inside out. Every possession of every resident had been checked. A handgun and two switchblades had been found, but no hint of drugs.

"Padmasvana was very distressed," Chupa-da said.

"I can imagine."

"No, I do not think so. He was not upset, because the young Penlop moved on to the next level of consciousness. Each of us has his karma. Padmasvana was concerned for the ashram. There was much publicity, in newspapers, on the television. That frightened people. It kept them away from the temple—people who would have been helped." Apparently my skepticism showed, for Chupa-da hurried on. "Because of his actions, the young Penlop was guilty of denying this opportunity to others. Padma graciously chose to assume and expiate this guilt so the young Penlop would not carry it to his next incarnation."

I said nothing. Suddenly, I felt very tired and sad. In those few minutes I had seen Padmasvana standing onstage I had been drawn to the man. His eyes, that caring expression, the sense that he was talking just to me, affected me as it had his followers. And I had seen the terror on his face as he clutched at the knife. I wanted more than a holy cover-up. I wanted to find the person who had come up though the trapdoor and coolly waited to stab Padmasvana.

Recalling that the altar was not at the center of the stage—where one would expect to find it—but at one side, directly over the trapdoor, I asked, "Who arranged the position of the altar?"

It took Chupa-da a moment to make the transition. He half smiled. "That is the task of the housemother, Leah deVeau," he said, a bit too eagerly. "She is here in the ashram. I will take you to her."

Chapter 4

But Leah deVeau was under sedation. No chance of a coherent word for at least twelve hours. I had an idea I knew who she was—the gray-haired, red-robed woman in the front row of the audience who'd had hysterics when Padmasvana died. It was frustrating not to be able to interview her now, but there were other things to attend to.

Even though I had been off duty when the murder happened, this case would be mine. In Berkeley, the beat officer first on the scene is responsible for any crime committed on that beat, be it littering or murder.

There were changes in the wind, however. A homicide squad was being formed and soon they would take charge, officially, of all murder investigations. So this might be my last chance to handle a homicide, and I was determined to make the most of it.

I would get assistance from my fellow beat officers, and there would be patrol officers too new to have beats of their own—like Connie Pereira—assigned to help me, but the responsibility would be mine.

The patrol officers had rounded up the Penlops and begun the tedious process of questioning.

The red-robed boys squatted along the walls of the dining room like boxes waiting for the movers. Most of them had their eyes shut, but even in repose their hard, drawn faces recalled the drugs and violence of their earlier lives. Was that violence gone or merely submerged by the lack of sleep?

I stepped outside a minute and took several deep breaths of the damp November air. The devotees had gone now, and only the squeals from the radios broke the silence.

Sometimes still, the world I worked in seemed unreal. Some of the male officers had dreamed of being cops for years, but not me. I had gone to college, bummed around Europe and met Nat. By the time Nat and I had married, he had been accepted in graduate school at Berkeley, and I had started looking for the perfect job.

The search had dragged on. My family offered money. Nat's family wrote about his working part-time. Nat began to suggest I was too particular, and I started to wonder if I was capable of finding *any* job.

At that juncture, the patrol officer's exam was announced—women and minorities encouraged. I took it without hope. When I passed, it surprised me. It surprised everyone. And when I started the job, kept it and actually found I did it well, the surprise took on a warm glow.

But police work is hard on marriages, even the most stable and traditional, where wives are willing to wait up till shift ends and understand that overtime is part of the job. Nat had his own life at school, his own demanding hours. The strain was too great.

Still, when the break came, it left a gaping hole.

I was glad, now, when cases ran late.

Taking a final breath, I turned back toward the ashram. A cry came from the darkness behind me.

It wasn't so much a cry as a howl, and it sounded like a baby. I shone my light to the left, across the grass and over the shrubbery. By the wall at the farthest point from both the temple and the ashram was a tepee, an Indian tepee!

Had I not just left the ashram cells, the tepee might have looked strange, but in comparison with those narrow cubicles its ten-foot diameter seemed spacious. As I walked toward it, the cries grew louder.

"Hello," I said, trying to make my voice heard over the baby's noise. "Hello!" Then I lifted the tepee's flap and stared. Inside it looked like a suburban tract-house bedroom—down to the pink-and-white crib and the makeup mirror on the dressing table.

"I'm Officer Smith," I said to the woman who stood by the crib clutching the baby.

"I don't give a damn who you are. Go away." She was in her early twenties, with long sandy hair, a tense set to her mouth and a sequin-trimmed cowboy outfit. It sparkled in the light. The baby was wrapped in a blanket, and all I could see were a few dark hairs.

"There's been a murder here."

"Yeah, don't you think I know? You think it's been silent tonight? Why do you think this kid's screaming, huh?"

At that, the baby started up again.

I waited till the cries subsided a little. "Has an officer talked to you?"

"Nah, they just tramped by."

"Okay." I took out my pad. "Why don't you start by telling me who you are?"

She plopped the baby in the crib. "Look, I don't want to start anything now. It's after midnight."

I took a breath. "Like I said, this is a murder investigation. You don't have a choice of answering or not. The only choice is how difficult you want to make it."

When she didn't respond, I softened my voice and said, "It's after midnight for me, too, you know."

Still she gave no reply. She glared, pulling her tweezed eyebrows tight over a pair of deep-set brown eyes. Her nose was straight, a bit too long, and her mouth pursed. She might have been attractive—not pretty—had her face not been scrunched up in anger.

"What's your name?"

"Heather. Heather Lee."

"And your child's?"

"Preston Lee. I named him after a jockey. I like horses." She aimed her glare at my face, waiting for my reaction. I displayed none.

"And you're one of Padmasvana's devotees?"

"A Penlop? Hell, no."

"Well, what are you doing here?"

"I live here."

"I can see that. Why do you live here?"

"They let me. You can't pitch a tepee just anywhere, you know. You got all these rules and ordinances and health and safety codes, and—"

"Who let you?"

"Rex."

"Why?"

"I asked."

"Heather! Why is Braga allowing you to stay here?"

"I told you."

I was getting nowhere. But this was a question I could take up with Braga. I glanced around the tepee. The sides looked sturdy, the poles—twelve in all—had been sunk solidly into the yard, and an inner canvas hung from them halfway down. The only light came from a marble oil lamp on the dressing table next to the crib. The table also held a mirror, bottles of makeup, nail polish, eyeliner, rouge—what any college girl might have on a dresser. Beside it was a portable radio, and hanging from the support pole were dresses, skirts, leather slacks—all of them expensive. I wanted to ask about them, but instead I said, "Where were you tonight?"

Her face had softened in my silence, but now the scowl returned. "Here."

"In the tepee?"

"Yeah."

"All evening?"

"Yeah, all evening. Where do you think you go with a kid that age?"

"You sure you weren't at the ceremony?"

"Listen, lady, if I was in there, with him"—she pointed to the sleeping infant "everyone would have known. And they would remember."

"You could have been there without him."

"I wasn't."

I could check that against the patrol officers' list of the members of the audience. I decided not to take the interview any further tonight. "I'll be back tomorrow," I said. "I want to talk to you then."

"Yeah, sure. I'm not going anywhere. The days of folding your tepee and stealing into the night are gone."

I headed back across the lawn toward the main building. Now the lights were out. I walked to the front. Leaning against the door was Howard, my fellow beat officer.

Seth Howard was his full name, but for him the "Seth" seemed superfluous. To one and all, Howard was Howard. A six-foot-six redhead, he looked like the archetypal Irish cop, right down to the grin. For any other cop, that quasi-humorous expression would have caused problems. But no one pushed Howard too far.

"What are you doing here?" I asked. Our shift had been over for nearly two hours.

86

"I heard you had a murder on your hands. I just finished a pile of dictation and I thought I'd see how come you got this one, when you're supposed to be off duty, yet."

I stared, trying to divine his motivation: professional interest or more?

Howard's beat covered the same area as mine—a square mile south of the campus inhabited by students and street people, and noted for its petty break-ins and drug traffic ranging from the sale of nickel bags to six-figure cocaine deals. We had handled a lot of drugs—too much. We'd both been glad when the word came down to lay off small-time marijuana. But murder was another thing. We didn't have many of those—maybe twenty a year in the whole city. And heading a murder investigation could look very good on an officer's record, particularly an officer who had visions of someday becoming chief. Like Howard. Like me. We had joked about our common ambition, but there was too much at stake for it to be entirely a joke. Beneath that superficial levity, I was keenly aware of our rivalry—he the cop's cop and me the woman cop in a city that prided itself on advancing minorities.

"I was at the ceremony when the guru was stabbed," I said.

"What?" Howard's curly red eyebrows rose. "You turning religious?"

"No. I know virtually nothing about Buddhism. A friend took me. She said it would be a good experience."

"Well, it will have been if you catch the killer before the Sunday papers go to press. If you let it go longer than that, it could be a very bad experience. There was a batch of reporters here when I arrived."

I glanced around. The complex was deserted now.

"Pereira gave them a statement and directed them to the

hospital," Howard said. "Then she let the rest of the guys go."

"Good. Did Braga clear out, too?"

"Him, too. His toupee was wilting."

"Damn. More questions have come up since I left him."

"You want to wake him? He only lives a few blocks away."

I considered the prospect for a moment. Heather's tepee rights would keep. "No."

"I've still got some work to do at the station," Howard said, resting one large freckled hand on my shoulder. "Why don't you clear up your dictation and then invite me to your place so you can tell me about this murder that I'm not going to get to investigate? I'll bring the liquid of your choice."

I hesitated, then said, "Make it Stolichnaya and you're on, but it'll take me a while."

As he glanced around my studio apartment looking for a place to sit, Howard's eyes rested momentarily on the right half of the room, which contained only my sleeping bag, a heap of books and a lamp resting on the floor. He settled on a wooden chair by the table. "Your husband got the furniture, huh?"

"I got the car. Neither was worth the fight. But the liquor cabinet's in good shape. What can I get you?"

He proffered a paper bag. "I brought your vodka, but you can give me bourbon if you have it."

"Bourbon it is."

Suddenly, it seemed disturbing having Howard here in my apartment, my sanctuary after the house with Nat had become a place I dreaded. Here, there were no surprises, no footsteps on the path foretelling the arrival of Nat and hours of bitter words or silences so tense every creak of the floorboards seemed to reverberate. No man had been here before.

Howard took the glass, positioned one ankle on his knee and leaned back. He'd changed out of uniform to a red plaid shirt that clashed with his hair. But it fit better than the regulation tan shirt.

"About your case . . . ?" he asked.

"It's an odd one. I mean, for me. I've seen bodies before, but I've never seen someone stabbed. . . . And that look of horror when he knew he was going to die . . ." My hand tightened on my glass.

The report that the lab had rushed to me had cleared up little. There were no prints save Padmasvana's, the remnants of his vain attempt to pull the knife from his chest. The knife itself was a cheap decorative item, but according to the report, the blade was five inches long, and it had been sharpened recently. The handle was the same length, gilded aluminum, and on it had been scratched a symbol that looked like a tick-tack-toe box with the extensions on the left and the top missing.

"Anyway," I went on, "there are plenty of people who could have done it: Braga; Chupa-da, the guru's assistant; Heather Lee; one of the Penlops. Any of them could have climbed up through that trapdoor and stabbed Padmasvana."

"Or anyone else on the grounds," Howard added. "It's lucky there's a high wall around the complex. At least that limits the suspects to people already there."

"Right. According to Pereira's report, the two Penlop boys at the main entrance swore no one left. The lab report didn't turn up anything to suggest anyone climbed the wall."

"It's not a wall you'd want to tackle; I had a look. It's ten feet high, smooth on the sides and jagged on the top."

I took another swallow of my drink. It was smooth and strong. "So who gains by Padmasvana's death?"

Howard sipped at his own drink, then set the glass down, his lantern chin jutting out as he considered the question. "What have you come up with so far?"

"First I thought of Braga, but there's no way he gains. He admits the gate was six hundred. Three ceremonies a week. Nearly two thousand. Not a fortune, but not bad. But once the guru's gone, so is business."

"Not necessarily."

"Huh?"

He held out his glass. "More bourbon will unlock the answer."

I got the bottle and set it on the table.

"The death of a leader," Howard said as he poured, "can be a real plus for a movement. Take Christianity, for example. Handled properly, with good PR, Braga could get a lot of mileage out of the guru's demise."

I swallowed the rest of my drink; it was an angle that hadn't occurred to me. "You're probably right; but Padmasvana would be a hard person to do without. He was very charismatic."

"All the better for the organization." Howard leaned back. "They've still got pictures. They've got memories. If he attracted people as much as you say—and I believe you, Jill; you're not one to get carried away—then they've got a lot of good memories working for them, memories that will only get better with time."

"Sure. Okay, Braga stays suspect. But what about the others?"

"The woman in the tepee?"

"Who knows? I don't even know who she is or why she's there. She doesn't show any interest in the activities. And I can't imagine Braga being touched by charity."

"Maybe she's got something going with him. That baby has to belong to someone."

"It's kind of an awful thought. Braga's so sleazy."

"There's a lid for every pot."

When I looked up, Howard grinned. "It's an old Howard saying," he explained, "handed down from Howard to Howard. An heirloom."

"No comment."

"Okay," he said. "What about the guru's assistant? Is he going to get promoted?"

"I don't know if the succession moves that way or if a whole new leader has to be found."

"Or maybe there will just be disciples."

"Right. But there's certainly a chance Chupa-da could benefit. Farfetched, perhaps, but not to be ruled out." I sat staring out the window. The moon was full. I could make out the shadow of the hedge in back of the yard. "I don't seem to be getting any further."

But if the hour and the vodka were fogging my mind, Howard's seemed to become sharper. And he seemed to have given a lot of thought to my case.

"Well, what about the method? It's not like he disappeared or was hit and run. It couldn't have been a more public killing."

"He'd said things about going." My words sounded muddy.

"Going?"

I nodded. "Going."

Howard shook his head, puzzled. "So then, who would gain by the guru's being stabbed in public? His public 'going,' so to speak."

I thought about Braga and Chupa-da and Heather and the

sedated housemother whom I hadn't talked to yet. "Under the circumstances, I can't see who. Unless . . . unless Chupa-da is going to succeed him. Then, instead of an obscure leader's dying and being followed by a more obscure one, Chupa-da has a lot of publicity when starting his reign. It doesn't sound very Buddhist, though."

"Like you said, you don't know much about Buddhism, Jill."

"I will tomorrow. I'll see Chupa-da first thing after the staff meeting. Maybe he can tell me about the markings on the knife, too."

Howard looked up questioningly, but I was too tired to explain.

I stifled a yawn. "You want another drink?"

Before he could answer, the phone rang.

Chapter 5

It was nearly noon when I awoke Thursday. Slowly the events of yesterday filed into my mind—the murder, the hours of interrogations, Howard drinking bourbon at the table and the 3:00 a.m. phone call from Nat.

The memory of my fury and awkwardness had prevented all but the most superficial suggestion of sleep. He had tried to call earlier, Nat had said. "It's three in the morning," I snapped. "That gave you a range." And what was it that couldn't wait till daylight? A death in the family? An act of God? (But I hadn't said that, not in front of Howard.) The Cost Plus stainless, that was it. Nat couldn't face another breakfast without it. "Try toast," I'd said and depressed the receiver—quietly; Howard was just leaving. And when Howard was gone, I pulled out the plug from the jack. Maybe I did have all the stainless. There were a couple of cartons in the kitchen I'd randomly thrown things in when I moved out. But I wasn't going to go through them at 3:00 a.m.

Now I pushed myself up, wandered to the kitchen and reheated the coffee. The dishes glared up from the sink. I rinsed a cup. Filling it, I realized that I had more than two hours to myself—one of the advantages of working the afternoon shift. There were plenty of things I could do. I looked back at the sink. Plenty I *should* do.

I dressed, threw half the coffee down the drain and headed for the ashram.

The temple was empty, and I went on across the grass past Heather's tepee, to the Penlops' ashram. As I mounted the steps I listened for voices, but there was nothing to break the silence. The door was open, the hall empty. I turned the corner into the dining room and stopped.

There lining the walls were the Penlops, squatted down, wooden bowls held in left hands and right hands shoveling some sort of paste from bowl to mouth. They were so incongruous, those street-hardened faces in the monk's robes.

By the front wall near the door sat the gray-haired woman who had screamed in the audience last night. Her eyes were nearly as red as her robe; her loose skin was blotched; and perhaps as a lingering effect of the sedation, she appeared listless.

"I'm Officer Smith," I said to her. "Are you the housemother, Leah deVeau?"

She moved to the door. "Come outside. It sets a bad example for the boys if I chat in the ashram." She lowered herself onto the porch steps, leaning back against the railing. "I'll do whatever I can to help. I'm very upset. I loved Padma. He was a son to me. More than that. He was a father, too. I loved him." Her voice was shaky, but she held it under control.

When she looked up, I said, "Why don't you start with what you do here?"

"Pretty much what I've been doing all my life," she said slowly. "I keep the house running. I see that the meals are made. I make sure the boys are all right."

"And did you take care of Padmasvana?"

It was a moment before she said, "Not really, I would have if there'd been anything to do, but Padma, he cleaned his own cubicle, he washed his own robes, he even took his turn at kitchen duty."

"And you are a follower of Padmasvana?"

"Oh, yes. In my own way. I can tell, dear, that that seems strange to you. I guess it is strange, particularly when the others follow such strict rules. But, you see, they need those rules. They're still children, really. Oh, they complain sometimes, and I have to talk to them. But I know that deep down, rules and certainty are what they need. Most of them have spent more time on drug trips in the last five years than they have straight. They need to be grounded. That's what Padma and I did." Her face paled at the mention of his name, and for a moment I thought she would break down. But she drew in another breath and said, "I don't mean to suggest that I am equal with Padma; I just mean that I am a mother to these boys. It's something I'm good at. You know, dear, when you're divorced at fifty-three and you've never worked, you're not prepared for much."

I said nothing. It did occur to me that Leah deVeau was one of those women who seem to exist to nurture. But her view of her charges as "children" was not confirmed by their hardened faces.

"I was very fortunate to find Padma when I did," Leah went on. "If I weren't here, maybe I would be a clerk in budget dresses or a counter lady at Woolworth's. And there'd be those awful lonely nights." She shook her head, as if trying to rid herself of the thought. "My husband wasn't much company, particularly in those last years, but there's a big difference in knowing someone else is coming home, regardless of who it is, as opposed to seeing the days stretch before you, endlessly uninterrupted—like a desert."

I, too, had been afraid of that once. But my days *hadn't* stretched before me like so much sand. I had volunteered for overtime. I had read books I'd been putting off for years. I had gone to meetings, and lectures and, yes, ceremonies that didn't interest me.

I changed the subject. "How did Padmasvana come here, to Berkeley?"

Leah deVeau seemed relieved, too. Taking a breath, she said, "Mr. Braga found him in Bhutan."

"Why was Mr. Braga in Bhutan?"

"I don't know. I'm really rather vague on this. All I know is that he was directed to Padma by an Indian guru—I forget his name—Indian names all flow together for me. Then Mr. Braga convinced Padma that his calling was in the West." She pressed the nail of her left thumb between the fingers of her right hand.

"Did you know he spoke some English?"

Again she paused, the thumb still pressed between the fingers. I found the nervous mannerism distracting. "Yes," she said.

"How much did he know? Did he talk to the boys?"

She pressed the thumb harder. "In the ashram, the boys— the Penlops—are supposed to speak only when absolutely necessary, and then mostly to me."

The door opened and four red-robed Penlops filed out, pausing by Leah deVeau. Three, although differing in height and coloring, had the unmistakable mark of the Penlops—the bleary-eyed shuffle. I recalled one of them from a burglary on Telegraph a year or so ago. He'd been fifteen then, a juvenile. But the fourth Penlop, a blond, was alert, wary.

It was he who said to Leah, "We're going to sell the tea. We're behind."

Sure, I thought. And what else? But if Leah recognized his intention, she gave no sign. She smiled and said, "Don't go for too long this time. You boys had a hard time last night.

Maybe you should stay . . ."

The blond put a hand on her shoulder. "No, Ma, we have our jobs."

Behind his urgency to get out of the ashram, I could see a genuine fondness in his expression. Leah deVeau's ministrations had not gone unappreciated.

As they crossed the grass, looking from the back like true Buddhist monks, I said, "It's hard to imagine these boys never talking at all."

A smile flickered among the creases of Leah's face. "It's hard for them, too. They haven't been used to an internalized life. Their lives have been spent totally in groups—peer pressure all the way." The smile broadened. "They have lapses. Some nights I hear whispers and even muffled laughter. Like the nights when my son had friends sleep over. I always heard them, even over my husband's sneezing—he had terrible hay fever. . . . But I'm wandering. These boys here, they do try, and they work hard."

"I'm sure they do," I said. "You know, one of the things I wanted to ask you was about the altar. I understand you arranged it."

The lines in her face tightened. "Arranged it?" She shifted her plump body on the step. I wondered if she was buying time. "The altar," she said, "is a replica of the one in Padma's monastery in Bhutan. He was already using it when I came here."

"But its position—it's not at the center of the stage. You decided that, didn't you?"

"What?" She stared at me, her face pale. "Oh, no, you don't mean . . ." The words came slowly. "The trapdoor."

I nodded.

"Oh, no! You mean someone used the trapdoor? Padma didn't kill himself? Someone came up through the trapdoor and stabbed . . ." She clutched her head, sobbing.

I waited and, when she wiped her eyes, said, "You did put the altar over the trapdoor, didn't you?"

"Yes." Her voice caught.

"Why?"

"It made sense at the time. I never dreamed anyone would . . . I just thought it was dangerous having that trapdoor on the stage. The temple is an old building. It hasn't been kept up. The boys can get careless when they're cleaning the stage. They run; they jump. I was afraid one of them would land on the trapdoor and fall through. I could see one of them breaking an arm or a leg. But I never . . . If I'd ever thought. But there was no reason to think of something like this. Who would want to stab Padma?"

"That's what I've been wondering."

"I don't know. I just can't imagine anyone intentionally harming Padma."

I stood up, and Leah deVeau pushed herself up to face me, a weary movement.

"This schedule must be hard on you, Mrs. deVeau. It really isn't meant for . . ."

"For old ladies?" She smiled. "The ashram's schedule isn't, but we do have other ways here. We have quite a number of older devotees. Mr. Braga seeks them out, and he sees to it that they are not pressed beyond their capabilities. That's one of the things that separated Padma's ministry from so many others." A yawn escaped her. "Sometimes I envy their schedule."

"I would have thought," I said, moving down a step, "that if some sort of salvation is the goal, the older you are the faster you'd have to work and the more strenuously."

Leah shook her head. "I don't know, dear. You'd have to ask Mr. Braga or Chupa-da, our new leader—he's the one to tell you about doctrine. I just keep the house."

I stopped. "Chupa-da's already the new leader?"

"Yes. He succeeded Padma."

"Does he hold the position in his own right? I mean, is he the new guru, or is he just a caretaker?"

"I can't say exactly. As I told you, it's not really my domain, the spiritual side. Chupa-da's in charge now . . ."

I followed her eyes as another line of Penlops snaked out of the ashram, tucking their wooden bowls into horizontal folds of red cloth over their stomachs. The resulting potbellies gave them the look of a row of red penguins. I turned back to Leah in time to catch her maternal smile as she watched them.

"I need to see Chupa-da," I said.

"He's upstairs." She didn't move. She looked very tired. "He's in the study. On the third floor."

There was a long pause before she added, in a tone of finality, "Padma used it as his room before I was here. He came to see it as unsuitable, so he moved down to one of the cells."

I hurried up the stairs, past those tiny cells, to a second staircase that led steeply to what had once been an attic. I knocked on the carved surface of the door, and hearing what could loosely be construed as "Enter," I pushed it open.

The room ran the length of the building, with windows at either end, but the real illumination was provided by a plastic skylight ten feet in length. The sunlight sparkled off deep-red Oriental rugs and burnished brass tables. A daybed stood opposite a desk, at which sat Chupa-da, looking like a clerk in a Turkish-rug emporium.

He turned his head toward me as I entered, mouth curling down, ruining the line of his round face. "We have no need of an investigation," he said, in the same singsong delivery of the previous night.

"Your leader has been murdered."

"No." His voice was uninflected. "Padmasvana's karma is complete. Nothing is permanent. We come. We go."

"I'm sorry, but the laws of California require that murder be investigated. We don't want to interfere with the operation of the ashram, but we must have your cooperation with our investigation." I found myself unintentionally mimicking Chupa-da's slow, precise speech.

"The days after the passing of a great leader must not be spent in the world but in contemplation of his wisdom and in marking well the lessons to be learned."

I thought about the Penlops, out selling tea as usual, but said only, "We will interfere as little as possible, provided you cooperate."

He glared at me with what could only be called a very unholy expression, then stood up. "Padmasvana," he said slowly, "was—what is your word?—harassed by Westerners. It was his karma to come here, to help the unenlightened, but they did not make it easy for him. They *wanted;* all of them *wanted* all the time. They did not understand that to be enlightened is to *not* want. All the time, they *wanted.*"

"Who wanted what?"

"Names? Braga. He wanted more ceremonies—what you would call an assembly line."

"Why?"

"To get more converts."

"And did Padmasvana do the extra ceremonies?"

"No!" Chupa-da's eyes flashed. "Padmasvana was part of a tradition that goes back many incarnations. It was not up to him to make changes."

I realized that I was still standing in the doorway and had felt no unspoken invitation to enter.

"And the real-estate man—he was here, sneaking about because Braga had banned him from the premises."

"What did *he* want?"

"Our land! The very temple we use for worship."

"And his name?"

Again the glare. "I do not know. I did not want to know." He gave a sharp flick of his head. "And the merchants, they accosted the Penlops when they sold tea in the street. They complained—me, mine, my business, my sidewalk. In this country people cannot walk along the street without merchants saying they walk on their land." Slamming down his hands, he added, " 'Don't sell tea in front of my store.' They complained from stores on Telegraph Avenue. The peddlers who sell their goods from blankets there complained about their space. They said you must go on the computer to get space on Telegraph Avenue—to sit on the sidewalk!" He sat back hard in his chair. "And the Co-op market. The Self-Over man. And—"

"The Self-Over man? Uh, Kleinfeld?" I said, the surprise showing in my voice. "But he runs self-awareness courses. Why would he care about selling tea?"

"No, no, not the tea. He complained about the Penlops speaking to people outside his studio."

It took me a minute. "You mean encouraging people to come to hear Padmasvana?"

"Yes. This is freedom of speech, yes?"

I nodded.

"The Self-Over man came here. He pushed into our building. He had to be removed by the Penlops." Chupa-da's dark eyes zeroed in on me. "The Penlops know how to remove intruders."

He turned his attention back to his desk, as though dismissing me.

I decided to ignore his last comment. "One more thing." I walked over to him and flipped back in my note pad until I came to the copy of the markings on the knife. "What does this mean to you? What does it look like?" I hoped that Chupa-da would announce that the symbol was an ancient Bhutanese figure pointing to the possessor of the knife and the killer of Padmasvana.

Chupa-da pushed the note pad aside. "Nothing."

"Does it look like a Bhutanese letter? A Buddhist symbol? Remember, the lettering could be inexact, careless. Look again." I placed the drawing before him and leaned on his desk as he looked at it.

He said, "No. It means nothing."

There were still things I wanted to know. Confronting Chupa-da had left me with more questions than I had begun with. Now it promised to be an exercise in diminishing returns.

But Self-Over touted increased awareness. Perhaps its founder would like to increase mine.

Chapter 6

From the blue-and-green storefront jutted a carved-oak sign: Self-Over, Garrett Kleinfeld, Founder. Kleinfeld's ads had appeared in local publications for as long as I had been in town. He was a fixture of the self-improvement scene in Berkeley.

The door was open. I walked into a large carpeted room sprinkled with batik-print-covered pillows. On the floor were six people, seated and twisted to the right. The tall upright man with blond hair I took to be Kleinfeld. He circled each panting pupil, speaking in a voice that carried easily across the room.

"Straighten the right leg, tighten the buttocks, pull in the lower ribs. That's better, much better, Larry. Mary, watch your back, it's beginning to arch; be careful not to lose the leg."

I moved closer, attracted by Mary's impending catastrophe.

"Jackie, breathe into the pose, don't hold your breath. Okay, release."

Sighs and pants greeted the command. The students untangled their legs and bent forward, reaching for their toes. Kleinfeld walked toward me with the buoyancy of a dancer. He was at least six feet tall, and although thin, his arms and legs showed muscles. Dressed in a T-shirt and shorts, his body could have passed for that of a college student, though I would have guessed him to be about thirty-five.

"Can I help you?" he asked.

"Garrett Kleinfeld?" When he nodded, I said, "I need to talk to you about Padmasvana."

The wrinkles in his brow deepened. His forehead creased and lines descended around his mouth. His was a mobile face. Its lines had formed a picture of calm command while he dealt with the students. Now the lines pulled against themselves into a pattern of wariness.

"This class is scheduled for fifteen minutes more," he said. "The students will go into the shoulder stand, and then the corpse."

The shoulder stand, I thought, must be very taxing, indeed.

Kleinfeld glanced back at them and then to me. "Would you prefer to come back or to hold your interview in the far end of the room once the posture is set?"

"I'll wait."

"Shoulder stand," Kleinfeld announced.

The six students adjusted blankets under their backs and wriggled around on them. Legs rose, hands pressed against backs, feet swayed in the air, until all six were still and in various degrees of verticality.

Kleinfeld moved among them, glancing up and down their bodies, occasionally standing behind a student and pulling him up by his legs.

When he had assessed and aligned all six, he returned to me, lowered himself to the floor, sat cross-legged and asked my name. I answered, and he repeated, "Jill. Sit down, Jill. The floor is all I have to offer."

After two-and-a-half years on the Berkeley police force, I

was used to conducting interviews on the floor.

Kleinfeld extended his legs and laid his torso out over them, so that his chin rested on his shins.

To the top of his head, I said, "Self-Over's been in Berkeley a long time. I would have expected to find more than six students here."

He hesitated.

"This is an introductory body class," he finally said. "It's not mainstream Self-Over. And not everyone is free at one-thirty in the afternoon. I've had as many as fifty students in the course."

I wished I could see his face. For someone who advertised that he would bring his students to the physical and mental condition where they would "not merely cope but walk lightly atop the world," he was rather defensive.

"What other classes do you have?"

Clasping his hands around the bottoms of his feet, he pulled. "The introductory classes are in Body Work, Nutrition for the Bay Area, Psychic Awareness in Daily Life. The main program brings together these and more subtle factors, which would take me considerable time to explain. It requires a total commitment, from my students and from myself."

"And that's what you've had fifty people in?"

"Yes."

Before I could comment further, he was on his feet instructing the class to lower their legs over their heads. Twelve legs descended. Kleinfeld walked behind the students, pushing backs straighter, tapping bent knees. Then he spoke again, and the legs raised slightly, the backs unrolled and the legs extended up, then forward till the students were lying flat on their backs.

"Corpse pose," he said. "Then, when you feel within yourself the time is right, leave in silence."

When he returned and settled into his previous pose, I asked, "Where were you last evening, after eight?"

"You mean when Padmasvana was killed?" Glancing up at me uneasily, he added, "I heard about it on the radio."

"And where were you?"

He jutted his legs out to the sides, so that they formed nearly a hundred-and-eighty-degree angle. Perhaps, I thought, if you were often in the company of body-awareness types, you got used to seeing this pose a foot in front of you.

Kleinfeld pulled back on first one thigh, then the other, making adjustments and, doubtless, using the time to plot out his answer.

"I was with a friend, a woman friend. Before you ask who, I'll tell you I can't answer that. She's married."

"Mr. Kleinfeld, this isn't the nineteenth century."

He sat up straighter, eyes pointed over my shoulder. "I'm sorry."

"All right, for now. Tell me about your problems with Padmasvana. I understand you were forcibly evicted from the ashram."

He bent his torso forward, planting his forearms on the floor in front of him. "I'll tell you about Padmasvana and Rex Braga and the crew. Yeah, I got tossed out of there, and I'd go back and risk the same thing ten times if I thought it would help. The whole bunch is a pain in the ass. Look out the door. Now, go ahead, now."

I got up and went to the door as two students slipped into their sandals and exited. In the middle of the path was a Penlop. There was no way for the students to avoid him. They accepted literature, nodded and escaped when the boy's attention was attracted by a third student coming toward them. This woman wasn't so fortunate. I watched for several minutes before she was able to extricate herself.

To Kleinfeld, I said, "Why didn't you contact the police if it's that much of a problem?"

"I would have looked bad."

"As if you were afraid of Padmasvana's appeal?" He gave me a grudging nod.

"So you went to the ashram?"

"Yeah, I went there . . ."

"When?"

He slid his legs under him, knelt and planted the top of his head on the floor, rounding his back forward till it formed a nearly perfect arc.

I repeated, "When?"

"Sometime last year." His voice was muffled.

"What time?"

"About this time. About a year ago."

"Around the time when the boy died there?"

He was silent.

"Mr. Kleinfeld, sit up and answer my questions."

He unrolled slowly, and when his face became visible, it was clear he had had time to decide on an answer.

"Yes. It was shortly after that."

Now I hesitated, then decided to go with my feeling. "You knew the boy who died, didn't you?"

Kleinfeld paused, then nodded. "Yes, dammit. I knew Bobby Felcher." The lines around his mouth pulled down hard in anger. "Yes, Bobby'd come here for the body class. He'd taken it on and off. He was on something—not heroin, probably reds. He was too hooked on whatever it was to get much out of body work. You need a steady base and good concentration. But maybe if he'd kept at it he could have shaken the habit; I don't know. I don't even know what possessed him to come here in the first place."

"What did happen to him?"

"He got caught by one of those goddamn Penlops. The next thing I knew, he wasn't coming here anymore; he was over there, living in their goddamn ashram. And then he was dead."

"The report says he brought the stuff in himself."

Kleinfeld's fists hit the floor. "So what does that prove? What kind of a place is that? A kid OD's and no one notices?"

"And then you went to the ashram?"

"Not right away. I was outraged, but there was nothing to do. No, I went there when they co-opted my next student. I went over there and found the kid, told him he was abandoning his potential, he was becoming . . . a tool. That's when they threw me out."

"And the student?"

"He stayed. His 'self' is a mere shadow now. I've seen him." Kleinfeld's face was red, and nothing so well described his tone of resentment as "sour grapes."

"I thought," I said, trying to disguise my tone of irony, "body work brought some sort of balance—that you wouldn't be so disturbed by life?"

I watched as he struggled to put together an answer. "It does," he said at last, meeting my gaze with difficulty. "For me, this is calm. Before I started I was angry all the time. I was discharged from the army because I nearly killed my sergeant." Noticing my expression, he added, "Don't worry. That was years ago. I'm under control now. I run, too. Five miles a day."

I nodded, and changed direction. "Do you know much about Buddhism?"

"Some."

"Tell me about it."

"What about it?" A flicker of irritation was apparent.

"The Buddhist attitude toward death."

"You want to know what they'll do with Padmasvana's remains? Well, they won't follow the practice of the Himalayas."

I waited.

"In the Himalayas, they don't bury the dead; the ground's too hard, mostly rock. They dissect the body and feed the organs to the vultures."

I shrank back.

"It's the only sensible thing. Dead is dead. It beats rotting underground."

I decided not to pursue that line of thought.

I glanced at my watch. I was cutting it close. "What *do* you think the ashram will do with Padmasvana's body?"

Kleinfeld smiled, a sarcastic smile. "Braga will arrange to milk it for everything he can get. He'll run the funeral as long as the health department lets him keep the corpse above ground. Then he'll start memorial services. If Rexford Braga had known the financial possibilities, he probably would have killed Padmasvana long ago."

"Are you accusing Braga?"

"No, no. I wouldn't put it past him, but I'm not pointing the finger."

"What do you know about Braga?"

Kleinfeld stood up and I followed suit. "Not much," he said. "I never heard of him before he opened shop here. Or of Padmasvana. Someone said Braga came up from L.A. There he could have been into anything."

I closed my notebook.

"You want some tea?" Kleinfeld asked, catching my eye and smiling disarmingly. "I could even come up with a Danish."

I hesitated. This was not among the standard offers made to cops, even in Berkeley. But, although the mention of a

Danish made me realize I was hungry, I wasn't about to spend another half hour with Garrett Kleinfeld—not on my own time. "Thanks, but I'm already late," I said, moving out the door.

As I tried to get my car engine to turn over, I wondered about Kleinfeld and his apparently strained financial condition. From the sound of his invitation, he was living in some corner of his studio. How much had Padmasvana cut into his livelihood? And he had nearly killed a man once. How much would it take now to push that temper to the point of stabbing?

Chapter 7

By the time I got to the station, the staff meeting was over. Officers were straggling away from the long table, grumbling about the work left by Morning Watch, about the afternoon heat that would turn to damp cold as soon as the fog rolled in, about the wool uniforms, the lack of Maintenance on the patrol cars, the—

"Smith." It was Lt. Davis, the watch commander.

"Yessir. Sorry I'm late. I was interviewing a suspect—"

"Fine." His tone belied the word. "That doesn't excuse you from staff meetings."

"Yessir."

"I'll see you in my office. Bring your notes."

"Yessir."

Lt. Davis's glass-sided office was spotless. In a building that had been painted too infrequently to keep pace with the coffee spills, scuff marks and the general grime of three shifts of police officers, Lt. Davis's office sparkled. And he fitted right in. His uniform was starched. Wiry black hair topped his caramel-colored face, and no errant strand marred the line of his mustache. If the thought of promotion was a consideration to Howard and me, it was the air he breathed to Lt. Davis. As he well knew, when the captain's job became available, the prospect of a black man with a Master's degree would be almost more than Berkeley could resist. Still, the lieutenant was not one to take chances. He was a fanatic for detail and would not hesitate long before replacing an officer whose rate of progress didn't meet his standards.

As I sat down he tapped his finger on the desk. "What have you got, Smith?"

I started to review the case, but he stopped me. "I've read the reports."

"Well, then," I said, "this afternoon I saw Leah deVeau, the housemother, and Chupa-da, the guru's assistant. Padmasvana may have lived simply, but Chupa-da isn't doing anything to curb his taste for luxury." I went on to describe the attic room. "I asked him about the symbol on the knife."

Lt. Davis flipped through the reports until he came up with the one from the lab. Looking at the picture of the symbol, he asked, "What is it, some Buddhist sign?"

"Not according to Chupa-da. He says he's never seen it before."

"Check it out, Smith. It may be something he just doesn't know. Go to the library. There are plenty of Buddhist places here in Berkeley; check with them. Get in touch with the consulate." He leaned forward, fingering his mustache. "The consulate. Smith, the Indian Consulate in San Francisco has already called here, you understand?"

"The *Indian* Consulate?"

"Bhutan doesn't have a consulate. India handles its foreign affairs." He waved off any further comment. "Naturally the consulate keeps a close eye on news about nationals under its jurisdiction. They are very concerned. This is no family knifing. They'll be getting in touch with the monastery in Bhutan right away. You see what I'm saying, Smith? This has got to be cleared up quickly. You see the paper this morning?"

Without comment, Lt. Davis extracted the paper from his desk drawer and smacked it down in front of me. The headlines were: "Guru knifed in Berkeley." Beneath was a picture of Padmasvana. The smaller print said, "Police Say No Leads."

The lieutenant eyed the smaller print, his lips turning down. "Not good. For today, Smith, *I* will deal with the press. I expect you to get me something to tell them."

"Yessir."

"Smith. You've got Pereira. Howard can assist. What else do you need?"

"Nothing right now, sir. It's under control," I said with more certainty than I felt.

"One final word," the lieutenant said as I stood up. "This has got to be cleared up before Sunday. Now we've just got the newspapers and the consulate to deal with. By Sunday we'll have every church in Berkeley wondering if the police are giving them proper service. You see what I'm saying?"

"Yessir," I said as I moved out the door.

When I got to my desk, Howard was there.

"Where's Pereira?" I demanded.

"You're in a grim mood."

"Pressure from above."

"Like I told you, Jill, this is no ordinary murder. The pressure'll only get worse."

"Thanks." I sat down. "Have you seen Pereira?"

"Connie went for coffee."

"Shit."

"It's not that bad." Howard grinned sheepishly. It was his pun look.

His mood was contagious. "I didn't mean to growl," I said. "Much as I would love a cup of coffee—even the Donut Shop's coffee—the last thing I need now is to have Davis spot me sitting here having a leisurely break."

"Okay, I'll drink yours. And what do you want me to do on the case? I've got time."

"Would you see what you can find on Garrett Kleinfeld, the Self-Over founder? And the temple?"

"You know I love research!" Patting my shoulder, he moved down the aisle.

I turned my attention to my in box, glancing through the papers, finding nothing new on the case. There were two frantic messages from Nat, but the stainless could wait. The whole set had cost only twenty dollars. I left a note for Pereira, asking her to see what she could find out on Braga from the LAPD, and to check the libraries for any clue to the marking on the knife, and headed downstairs to the motor pool.

For myself I had saved the questionable task of another visit with Braga himself. But when I arrived, the temple was still empty. As I headed across the yard to the ashram, I noticed the flap of the tepee was up.

"Hi," I said, poking my head inside. The tepee looked the same as last night, with the sleeping bag and pillow next to the vanity table that held the marble oil lamp. Only Heather was different. Instead of the sequined cowboy outfit, today she sported a Gypsy ensemble, with a neck-straining collection of gold chains.

"Hi," she said, making no effort to hide her irritation.

Again, I had the feeling that she might have been attractive had it not been for her seemingly permanent scowl.

"I see your baby's not here."

"Yeah. Leah's got the kid. I've gotta have time off. I can't be looking after that kid seven days a week. She takes him a few days."

"Nice of her."

"Well, I've gotta have some time to myself. It hasn't been easy, the last twenty-four hours."

Sitting on her vanity stool, I said, "This is a very serious crime, Heather. I need to know about everyone here. Why don't you start by telling me how you came to know Rexford Braga?"

"This is my afternoon off. Come around later when I have to be here, anyway."

"Heather."

"Okay, okay. I came to a ceremony."

"Here?"

"Yeah. I was in college back East. I came here for spring vacation."

"And Braga held the ceremony?"

"No, of course not. What could that old buzzard do? Padma held the ceremony, just like he always did."

"And so what happened to you?"

She pulled a lock of sandy hair in front of her shoulder and divided it into thirds to braid. "I got fascinated. That's how I met Braga."

"And then?"

Pulling her fingers through the braid, she loosened the hairs, redivided them and began the intertwining again. "Well, nothing, really. I just went to the meetings. Like I said, I was really into it. When the girl I drove out here with went back East, I stayed."

"And had the baby?"

"Well, not right away. Not till a year later."

"Heather, who is the baby's father?"

"What? Listen, what business is that of yours?"

"Heather." I sounded like my mother.

"Okay, okay. He was a guy passing through. His name was Lee." But there had been a pause before she gave the name.

115

"You were married, then?"

"Nah. I just took his name. It was better than my own."

"Which was?"

"Moore."

Obviously, a subtle difference. "And where can we find him now?"

Her scowl lines deepened. She opened her mouth and shut it again. "I don't know. I don't keep in touch. He was on his way to Mexico."

"You don't get child support?"

"Are you kidding? Would I be living in a tepee if some sucker were sending me cash?" She slipped the braid onto her shoulder, staring down at the escaping sprigs of hair.

"What about Chupa-da?" I asked.

"What do you mean? What about him?"

"Well, you say you were drawn by the religion. You must know something about the rules. Does Chupa-da automatically succeed Padmasvana? I mean—"

"What!"

"Well, Chupa-da's taken over Padmasvana's study, and he's acting head of the ashram, and—"

"He's in Padma's study? The one on the third floor?"

"Right."

"You said he was *acting* head?"

"As far as I know."

"Well, that damn well is all he is. He's got no more right to pretend to be the guru than you do, you hear me? And if he's saying anything else, he's got another thing coming!"

"Heather, are you saying Chupa-da's breaking the tradition?"

She stood up, ignoring my question.

"Heather, what is the tradition? Do you know?"

"What I know is that Chupa-da just better not think he can

step into Padmasvana's shoes!"

"Heather—" But she had rushed out of the tepee and was heading across the lawn to the temple.

I followed Heather, waited while she stormed into the temple and trailed after her as she burst out of the empty building and careered across the lawn to the ashram. Without a look she passed Leah, who was sitting on the porch holding the baby, and made for the stairs, nearly knocking over a dazed Penlop. Following her to the second-floor landing, I braced for the explosion when Heather would come upon Chupa-da.

But there was silence—broken only by a clumping of feet as Heather barged past me down to the porch.

"Where is he?" she demanded of Leah. As I descended, she added, "I can *see* he's not here!"

Heather loomed over Leah, hands on Gypsy-clad hips. Leah, still holding the baby, had the forbearing look of eternal motherhood.

"Calm down, Heather. Chupa-da's gone out. He doesn't tell me where he goes. He's the guru, not me."

"Guru! He's got no right. My son, Preston, has more right than him. Who does he think he is?"

Leah shrugged.

"Lot of good it does talking to you. You're one of them. You don't give a damn what happens here, as long as no one rocks the boat. You can just go on being mommy. Give me that kid. You can take your neuroses out on one less little boy!" She grabbed the baby, stomped down the steps and strode past the tepee to the street. In a moment, I heard the revving of an automobile engine and then the squealing of wheels.

Looking down at Leah, I asked, "What was all that about?"

Her head was bowed, her shoulders hunched over the empty space in her lap.

"You really care a lot about the baby, don't you?" I asked.

She nodded. "He's so little; he needs someone stable. Heather's just not ready to be a mother. She's only a child herself. It's an awful thing to say, but I'm surprised nothing's happened to him. It's not that Heather would ever hurt him, not intentionally; it's just that she doesn't have the maturity to think beyond herself. When she feels pressed, she puts up her defenses, and she's only got room for 'me.' "

Sitting down opposite Leah, I asked, "Why was she so outraged when she heard Chupa-da was acting head of the temple?"

"Because she doesn't understand."

I waited.

"Heather is very Western. She thinks that being a guru is like being president of General Motors—you have piles of money and endless power and prestige."

"And?"

"Bhutanese Buddhists believe that each person comes into this incarnation for a purpose and, if your purpose is to learn what's involved in being head of a temple, fine. But if you have to learn about being a janitor, that's just as important."

"But surely you must have to be holier than most people to be the guru?"

"You'd think that, wouldn't you?" She brushed off her skirt as if dusting off the remnants of her scene with Heather. The skin on her face was loose, and pouches sagged at either side of her mouth. She could never have been pretty, even as a young woman—her features were too big for her face. But her maternal expression softened their angles and created an impression of pleasant warmth.

She leaned back. "Padma said you must experience it all. It just happens to have been his job in this incarnation to be the leader."

"And Heather doesn't think that Chupa-da needs that experience?"

"No, no. Heather couldn't care less about Chupa-da or his karmic growth. She thinks there's gain to be had, and she wants it."

"Heather wants to be guru!"

"Oh, dear, I guess I'm not making myself plain. Heather wants to be regent, for her son."

I pulled out my pad and made a note. "So you're saying Heather wants her son—the baby—to be the guru. And she wants to run the place till he's of age?"

"Right. I guess I *am* making sense."

"Well, only to a point, I'm afraid. Why would Heather think her baby should be guru?"

"Succession."

"Succession?" I recalled something about deceased gurus being reincarnated, but I assumed that they had to be dead before their spirit moved to another body. For Heather's baby to be an embodiment of Padmasvana, one of them would have had to be without a spirit for nearly a year. "Heather doesn't strike me as that involved in religion to see her son as a reincarnation of Padmasvana."

"Oh, dear, now I'm not being clear again. That's what my ex-husband always said. I don't mean anything about incarnations or cosmic-ness or anything like that. I don't really understand it all, though I have made some effort. Despite what Heather says, she has made none. She does nothing but sit in her tepee and listen to country music on the radio. What Heather thinks is that Preston is the logical one to succeed Padmasvana."

At last I was beginning to catch her drift. Still, I asked, "Why?"

"Maybe you'd better have a look at Preston."

Chapter 8

Preston, of course, was off with his mother. Everyone in this case seemed to be absent when I wanted them. I tramped back to the temple for another try at Braga.

He, too, was still missing, but I did find Chupa-da. The robed Bhutanese was seated at Braga's desk, hunched over a pile of papers.

"Heather is very angry with you," I said, for openers.

Chupa-da looked up, only very mild signs of annoyance breaking through the blankness of his expression.

"She says you have no right to succeed Padmasvana."

"She is ignorant." He turned his attention back to the papers.

"Is Preston Padmasvana's child?"

His face flushed, but he controlled it before speaking. "Padmasvana was celibate. His mind was on things higher than . . . Heather."

"Then what is she doing here?"

"I do not know. Padmasvana in his wisdom let her remain."

I could see that I was getting nowhere. Moving closer to the desk, I glanced at the top paper, a list of names and amounts.

"Is that the contributors' list?"

He turned the sheet over. "This is the business of the temple."

"I want to see the books."

"You cannot."

"Of course I can."

Chupa-da hesitated. "The books are locked in the safe."

I nodded.

"Only Mr. Braga can open the safe. He has the combination."

"I'll wait."

From the strained look on Chupa-da's face, he was employing all his monastic training in order to preserve his equanimity. "There is nothing to see. The temple takes in money from contributors and from ceremonies. It is not much. We are many people. We have expenses."

"Such as?"

He took a breath. "We pay for our light, our heat, for the water we drink, for what we eat and for our robes. And we pay a large amount for the land and buildings."

"You're buying the land?"

"Not I. Not Padmasvana. Mr. Braga."

"Rexford Braga's using the temple's money to buy the land?"

Chupa-da nodded slowly. "It is the foolishness of the Western mind. In Bhutan we know that it is foolish to think that a little man can possess the earth. The earth and the rivers are like the air and the rain. But here men play a game with each other; they pretend they can possess the earth; they trade it back and forth, like children with trinkets."

Before I could speak, Chupa-da added, "This land is a sought-after trinket. Mr. Braga has been forced to evict the realtor seeking it. Mr. Braga ordered him to stay away."

We'd been over this ground before. I nodded. "And did

he? Stay away, I mean."

"At first, no. Each time the man came, a Penlop found Mr. Braga and Mr. Braga had the Penlops remove him. The realtor was always in the temple or inside the ashram. He was not hard to find."

"What was the man's name?"

"I do not know. I know him only to see him."

Glancing back at the desk, I said, "About those papers . . ."

"Wait. I will think. He was part of a company. Will that help?"

"It might."

"He is the age of Mr. Braga. He is not tall. He has little hair left. He has a very large nose and stomach."

"His company?"

"It is called Comfort."

"Okay, I'll check him out."

It was getting toward dusk as I drove across town. If I had been higher in the hills, I might have caught a glimpse of sunlight on the Bay; if I'd been in San Francisco, I could have seen the sun set over the Pacific. That thought always made me smile. When Nat and I had first come to Berkeley, he wanted to take me across the Bay of the Cliff House to see the sun set. Blasé, I'd asked why we should make a special effort when he had grown up on the East Coast and could have watched the sun set over the Atlantic anytime. Nat had been appalled when he'd realized I believed the sun set in the east.

But now, as dusk neared, my thoughts were on Comfort Realty. I hoped the offending realtor was an eager beaver and didn't close shop at five. Another missing witness I didn't need.

But Comfort Realty was an establishment even Lt. Davis would have approved of. Though the stores around were closing, it was brightly lit and, through the picture window, I could see the paunchy, balding realtor of Chupa-da's description.

The man's movements as he hurried to unlock the door belied his comfortable appearance. They were the nervous gestures of a nail biter. "Can I help you? Residential property?" He stared. "Oh, a policewoman. Nothing wrong, I hope?"

I followed him inside. The room was warm and the air stale. "I'm Officer Smith. I'm investigating the death of Padmasvana, the guru over by Telegraph."

"That son of a bitch." The realtor sunk into his chair and, grabbing a pen, began flicking the ballpoint in and out.

"Do you mean Padmasvana or Rexford Braga?"

"The whole lot of them. Pack of frauds, trapping kids with their mumbo jumbo."

"I understand you were kept off the premises."

"Yeah, can you believe it? That Braga thinks he's big stuff, but he's got no head for business."

I waited.

"Well, lady, I'll tell you what went down. See, that's a good parcel of land there. There ain't but one or two unimproved lots in all Berkeley. I could knock down that temple and the house in a couple of days. Cheap."

"And build."

A smile flickered briefly on the realtor's face and departed as if unsure of its welcome. He riffled through a drawer and smacked a paper on the desk in front of me. On it was an artist's conception of a ten-story apartment house with picture windows and wrought-iron railings, but essentially the shape of a refrigerator box. The sketch was complete, to the suggestion of plants in the upper units and lettering on the windows of the first floor.

One of Berkeley's great charms was its old houses: Victorians; brown-shingles tucked under live oak trees. Even less-antique frame cottages, painted salmon and rust or brown and violet, had their appeal. I shuddered as I imagined this monstrosity in place of the ashram. It could wreck the entire neighborhood.

"See," the realtor said, "we could all make a killing. Now look, lady, I've pulled no punches with these people. I told that fool Braga I'd pay him the market value for that lot. A hundred and twenty thousand is nothing to sneeze at. The guy's a fool."

"Did you talk to Padmasvana?"

"Nah. Wasn't for lack of trying. Believe me. I tried to get those red-robed page boys to let me in to see him. Once, I buttonholed the other monk. But everybody kept the big boy covered."

The phone rang. Nodding abruptly at me, he picked it up. "Yeah," he said. "Of course I'm still interested. I haven't been calling to talk weather. So what's what? No, I got to have more. Ninety or nothing. Look, if I could swing an eighty-percent loan, you think I'd be dealing with you? You're not as reliable as Bank of America, you know!" He listened a minute, sweat beading his brow. He glared at the tightly closed transom as if it were the person on the phone. "So check, already. You can tell them Vern Felcher told you to ask." He slammed down the phone.

"Vern Felcher!"

"Yeah, lady, Vernon P. Felcher. Who'd you think you were talking to?"

Was I losing my touch? What else had I neglected to ask? "Are you any relation to Bobby Felcher?"

Felcher's hands were still for the first time.

"Yeah, Bobby was my son. My only son. And if you're

going to ask how I feel about Paddy-what-sis getting his, I only wish I could have been the one who did it."

"Is that why you kept going there?"

"To kill him? Make sense, wouldn't it? But no. What I told you about the land is true. I want that land. I have a right to it. My son died there. He died because of them. I want to get that land and wipe out any trace of that bunch." Felcher's broad knuckles were white against the ruddiness of his hands. Sweat rolled down the side of his face, but he made no move to open the transom.

"Mr. Felcher, you said they were responsible for Bobby's death."

"Yeah. Those vultures. They lured him in there."

"How?"

"I don't know what they told him."

"He lived with you?"

"Only about a couple of months. I'm divorced. His mother had him before he came to me. She took him to her hometown—Visalia—in the San Joaquin Valley. We'd lived there when Bobby was small. He liked the town, he said. But as soon as he got there, he went wild. And she was too damned weak and woolly-headed to keep on him. By the time I got him, he was already up to his ass in drugs."

"What happened to Bobby after he came to stay with you?"

Felcher's fingers tapped on the edge of the desk. "Like I said, Bobby was in no great shape when he came back. We'd all lived in Berkeley before the divorce, so he knew all sorts of no-goods up on Telegraph already. I tried to keep tabs on him, but that isn't easy when you work the hours I do. And then he spent every other weekend with his mother, and she let him lie around and pop pills and God knows what."

"So Bobby spent a good deal of time on Telegraph?" That

supported what the Bobby Felcher file had said.

"Probably. He got home late. He slept late. I don't know what he did while I was working. Supporting him and paying alimony wasn't easy." Felcher leaned toward me, his heavy features stiffening as he waited for my nod. "I kept after him to do something constructive. Not school or anything as out of reach as that. Jesus, is it too much for a man to hope his only son would think about going to college? I work my ass off in this realty company. Bobby could have walked in here. He could have made forty thousand a year working part-time. You think . . . No. Not real estate. Not college. The kid couldn't even get through high school."

"You said you'd pressed him to . . ."

"Anything. Anything constructive. I tried to get him to work out, go to a gym like I used to do"— he glanced down at his stomach—"when I was thinner. It wasn't so long ago. I was built like Bobby—lanky. I exercised; I kept in shape. He did nothing but sit and stare and take pills."

"And so he went to Self-Over?"

Felcher froze.

"I've already interviewed Garrett Kleinfeld."

"Oh, yeah, well, he's no prize, either. But at least there, with him, Bobby was getting some kind of exercise and he was associating with a decent class of people."

"Oh?"

"You wonder how I know about Kleinfeld's setup, huh? I followed Bobby. I promised him twenty bucks a week if he did something. Vern Felcher don't spend money for nothing."

"And did it help?"

"Maybe a little; who knows. Maybe it would have, but about that time, he got involved with those damned Chinks."

"How'd he meet them?"

Felcher's face tightened. "Who knows? They're all over. What difference does it make?"

"So then . . ."

"Then he started going over there, and next thing he's living there, and then he's dead." He slumped back in his chair.

"Do you feel they were responsible for his death?" I asked more softly, hoping my question would converge with his thoughts.

"Yeah," he said. "I know everyone said he brought in the drugs. He probably did. But what kind of place allows that? What about that housemother, what was she doing?"

"The present housemother, Leah deVeau, wasn't there then."

Felcher leaned forward suddenly. "What? You . . ."

He seemed so startled and upset that I asked, "Did you think there had been a housemother then? Surely you knew there wasn't—"

"I don't care whether they had a housemother or—or not," he said. "They had no business letting my son overdose. Look, I work sixty hours a week. I'm never home, and Bobby didn't overdose here. What kind of a place are they running? Yeah, I'd like to wipe it off the earth."

I made a show of jotting notes, giving him time to cool down. Wiping perspiration from my brow, I asked, "Mr. Felcher, where were you last night between eight and nine?"

"At the movies."

"Which one?"

"The California. They were showing a Charles Bronson."

"When did it start?"

"Jesus, lady, you think I remember that!" His fists tightened, and I thought of how easily that meaty hand could have shoved the knife into Padmasvana's unprotected chest. "It was the first show. I was home by ten-thirty."

"Fine." I wrote: Cal—1st sh. Bron. The California The-ater had four theaters in one. Felcher would have had to come nude to be remembered. "Mr. Felcher, as a realtor, what would you guess the payments on the property would be?"

He leaned over, riffling through another drawer. "Don't need to guess," he said in a calmer voice. "Ain't no payments. Just property taxes."

"No payments?" That certainly wasn't what Chupa-da had told me, but perhaps he had mistaken the taxes for pay-ments. "Are you sure?"

"Yeah, lady, I'm sure. You don't make it in real estate with maybes. And believe me, I checked this place out. Some old idiot joined the group, willed them the property, then died. Before you jump, the old girl dropped dead from heart failure, brought on by years of diabetes—no funny business. Believe me, I checked. Left the whole goddamned place to them. Every penny paid."

"What would you guess utilities run in a place like that?"

Felcher flipped through his papers. "Last year, midwinter, sixty a month, including the temple. And most of that was for water. As far as I can see, they don't heat the house, but they can't keep the page boys from taking a leak."

I leaned on the desk. "You've given their operation a lot of thought, Mr. Felcher. If the money they take in isn't used for mortgage payments and utilities, where do you think it's going?"

Felcher leaned in, placing a hand on my arm. "You'd better ask that stuffed sausage of an emcee that question."

Chapter 9

Eager as I was to have a stab at the "stuffed sausage," I realized it had been seven hours since my practically nonexistent breakfast, and nearly five since Garrett Kleinfeld had filled me with longing for a Danish. In that time I had crossed Berkeley as regularly as a local bus driver. Surely there must be a more efficient way of investigating.

As I headed back to the station now I tried to organize what I had learned in those seven interviews. Heather had aspired to power in the name of her baby, but Chupa-da had beaten her to it. He had thrust himself in Padmasvana's place with what could only be viewed as unseemly haste. And he had lied about making payments for the temple lands. Or had Braga lied to him? An interesting thought. Was Braga pocketing money and telling Padmasvana's followers he was making monthly payments?

Braga? If indeed the property was in his name, with Padmasvana dead he could sell it to Felcher and clear one hundred and twenty thousand dollars.

And Felcher. For motive, he had it all: the completion of his dream, his ten-story monstrosity; a huge profit; revenge for his son's death.

I sighed as I got out of the car. In life Padmasvana had been an appealing young man. In death he'd become merely the means to satisfying a great deal of greed. And that led me back to the question of the temple's finances.

But now I headed inside the station to see who was interested in food.

My preference would have been Howard. My second choice would have been Connie Pereira. What awaited me would have been my last choice—Lt. Davis.

He motioned me in as I came by the glass partition of his office. As always, the cubicle was spotless, the papers on his desk in geometric piles, his red-plaid thermos aligned with the edge of the desk.

"Sit down, Smith."

I sat, taking out my note pad.

Placing his hands on the desk, he said, "So where are you with this guru thing? It's already Thursday night. By tomorrow the papers are going to be through milking the temple and the guru. Then they'll start on us. 'Why haven't the police found the killer? Are the cops harassing the temple?' They'll scream prejudice against Buddhists and Bhutanese, or maybe just plain incompetence. You see what I'm saying, Smith?"

"Yessir."

"So?"

"Well, I've been thinking about the temple's finances. They've been having two ceremonies a week, at five bucks a head. The night I was there the place was packed—about a hundred twenty people."

"Six hundred dollars," he said immediately.

"Twelve hundred a week. Contrary to what Chupa-da told me, there's no mortgage—someone willed them the property. Utilities and the type of food they eat couldn't run over five hundred a month. Make it a thousand, with clothing and light bulbs and the like."

"So they net forty-two hundred a month."

It was a moment before I trudged through the calculations for four-and-a-third weeks. "Yeah."

"And where does that forty-two hundred go?" I shook my head. "I hope Braga tells me, but somehow I can't believe it's so on the up-and-up that he'll be willing to publicize it."

The lieutenant sat, fingering his mustache. "Okay, Smith. Use what overtime you have to. I want this cleared up before it begins to smell, you understand? But watch you don't step on any toes over there."

"You're asking me to walk a pretty fine line."

"You can do it, Smith." He nodded and looked down at the top paper on his pile.

I stood up, basking in this rare expression of confidence. But if I wanted that confidence there tomorrow, I'd have to produce.

Half an hour later in Wally's Donut Shop, I wiped a dab of synthetic grape jelly from the corner of my mouth, swallowed the rest of the cup of sour coffee, paid Wally and headed back toward the temple. Pressed for time, I'd had to choose between dictating and food. The dictating machine, I'd figured, wasn't likely to growl in the midst of an interview.

As I came within a block of the temple, I heard a voice, the words unclear, bellowing over a loudspeaker. Cars were parked in every conceivable place—every corner curb was full, every red zone taken, every fireplug blocked. I double-parked.

The temple, likewise, was packed. All the seats were filled, the aisles were crammed with squatters, the walls draped with standees. If the candles sent the altar up in flames, not everyone would be able to escape in time.

Shutting the door behind me, I watched the proceedings.

The huge picture of Padmasvana behind the altar was framed by white draperies. Chupa-da sat on one raised seat. The other Padmasvanas—held a spray of lilies. Chupa-da was speaking in a singsong voice that droned past my consciousness with only an occasional word breaking through. Braga sat to the side of the stage in his white outfit, watching. I noted that his expression of interest looked forced.

The atmosphere of the room was different from my previous visit. Despite the mob scene there was none of the excitement of the last ceremony. The whir of the electric fans was barely audible over the swish of crossing and uncrossing legs.

Deciding to try for a better vantage point, I stepped back outside and circled the building till I came to the basement door. It was locked but, as I suspected, the lock wasn't much of a deterrent.

I made my way down the steps to the main basement room. Along all four walls piles of tea cartons loomed, and deep shadows draped off them. When Bobby Felcher died, there had been questions about all that tea and about Chupa-da's weekly supply run to Chinatown in San Francisco.

Above, the stage creaked.

Instinctively, my hand poised over my holster.

I moved slowly to the small door, part of the supporting wall of the stage. I would have had to bend to get through it; it was only four feet high. I pulled it in toward me.

I had intended the movement to be inconspicuous. The night I had been in the audience all twenty-four Penlops could have paraded through the door unnoticed. But tonight heads turned and eyes stared. My watchers appeared to be in no hurry to return their attention to the stage above me. Since the light in the basement room was off, I stayed motionless, waiting them out, and in a minute or two most people looked away though the performance above me failed to hold their interest and a disconcerting number kept glancing back at me.

I checked the room for familiar faces. Halfway back I spotted Ginny Daly. Her face was drawn, her eyes were pink and puffy from crying, and her frizzy hair hung limp. But her expression was one of boredom.

Looking across the aisle, I saw more faces like Ginny's—faces that bespoke the grief of Padmasvana's death. But they, too, had wandering eyes and mouths set in annoyance. I wondered how Chupa-da could fail to hold the attention of Padmasvana's devotees at this, of all times.

The only people whose eyes remained on Chupa-da were seated near the front on the far side of the aisle from my vantage point—Leah and Heather.

Overhead, on the stage, came a thump and footsteps. More clearly, I heard Chupa-da's voice. "Death," he said, in his singsong voice, "as you call it, is an extension of life. Life goes on. Life did not begin in this incarnation. It did not begin in the incarnation before this. It did not begin in the incarnation before that. It did not . . .

I turned my attention back to the two women. Leah, in her red Penlop robe, looked as worried as any mother when one of her boys was not doing well. Heather, dressed all in black, sat coolly appraising the debacle.

And in the rear of the audience, standing near the door, was Vernon Felcher. I couldn't make out his expression, but I could guess at it.

Felcher was glancing around the temple, probably calculating what the demolition would cost.

I looked for Garrett Kleinfeld, wondering if he, too, had been drawn to the ceremony, but he was not there.

I was about to close the door, when the clash of a gong reverberated above my head. The audience rose, and with a minimum of ado, the squatters in the aisles clambered up and began pushing toward the exit. They moved fast, except to the left of the door, where there was a delay of some kind. As I sorted out the bodies involved, I realized that the problem was caused by Vernon Felcher, fighting his way against the moving throng. He propelled his rotund person toward the front of the auditorium and, brooking no interference, made his way to the row where Leah and Heather sat. Here he stopped, and his expression changed from the single-mindedness that had moved there to a flush of anger. He leaned over the pair of seated women and spoke.

I stepped through the doorway into the temple.

Felcher moved past Heather and stood looming over Leah.

I pushed through the crowd toward them, but even in uniform I didn't have the success that the obstreperous realtor had enjoyed. When I reached the center aisle I could see their faces—Felcher's angry, his mouth moving rapidly; Leah's fearful. Felcher leaned down and grabbed Leah's arm. She jerked it away. Heather stood up. Still talking, Felcher pushed her back in the chair.

Braga appeared behind him with two large Penlops. The red-clad figures grabbed Felcher and dragged him to the aisle, where Braga cleared a path. In another minute, Vernon Felcher had been thrown out of the temple again.

"What was all that about?" I asked as I came abreast of the women.

Heather looked at Leah.

Swallowing, Leah said, "That was Vern—Vernon Felcher . . ."

When she didn't continue, I asked, "What did he want?"

"I don't know, I've never even talked to him before." She

looked down a moment, pulling herself together. "I guess you know he was Bobby Felcher's father."

"Yes."

Heather stood up. "That man's caused us a lot of trouble. I didn't think he'd have the nerve to come here, not now."

"What did he want?" I repeated.

"He probably just wanted to make trouble," Heather said. "He grabbed Leah's arm. Did you see that? Look, you can still see the marks. He said, 'So you're the housemother. Where were you when Bobby needed you?' I mean, Leah wasn't even here till months after Bobby died. That man's crazy, and he's dangerous. Look what he did to Leah's arm!"

I looked. The marks were still visible. I recalled Felcher's meaty hands, and I thought how unpleasant it would be to be caught by them.

"Has he done anything like this before?" I asked Heather.

"Nothing physical. I mean, he never got the chance. But he threatened a lot. He threatened Chupa-da. That was at first. Then he got a lot calmer. I guess when he decided to buy the temple he figured he'd better cool it. But you can see how dangerous he is, can't you? Who knows what he would have done if the Penlops hadn't stopped him?"

Leah said nothing. Her face was still white. Her hands quivered against her thighs.

The temple was empty now. "Why don't you take Leah to her room," I suggested to Heather.

As I made my way to my car I wondered about Vernon Felcher. Maybe Heather was right. Maybe he was crazy. There had been no reason for him to attack Leah. He knew she hadn't been at the ashram when his son died. I had told him that myself.

I called into the station and left a long memo for Pereira, filling her in on most of what I'd learned that day and asking her to check out the relevant parts of it in her interview with Braga. She could handle Braga and his books alone. Whatever secrets the temple's accounting system hid Pereira would ferret out.

I headed the car north along Telegraph, briefly considering whether I should call in again and get Felcher's home address. Or should I check Comfort Realty first? It was after ten; there was no reason for Felcher to go back to work, but the office was close and I circled by.

The lights were on, the door unlocked. I walked in. Felcher was seated in his desk chair, thumbing through the Multiple Listing book as he might a magazine in the dentist's office. On the desk was a cup half-filled with dark liquid that smelled like Scotch.

"This is my office; that's what I'm doing here," Felcher said in response to my question.

"You could have gone home."

"Yeah. I could have. I didn't." He took a drink, put down the cup and fingered his ballpoint pen.

I leaned on the arm of the client chair. "What was that scene about at the temple? Why were you threatening Leah deVeau?"

"Threatening?" He raised his eyebrows. "I was just reminding them about their shoddy operation and about what they did to Bobby. I don't intend to let them forget Bobby."

"But you knew Leah wasn't there then."

"So? She's there now. She's part of the operation." He took another drink.

"Is that all you've done, threaten?"

"Yeah, and it's a shame. I know where you're leading. But if I'd done in Paddy Guru I wouldn't be downing Scotch or tramping over there to scream at those bums. I'd be sitting back with a big smile on my face."

To a degree, that made sense. I slipped into the chair I'd been propped against. Obviously, Felcher cared about his son. But how much? And what form would his grief and anger have taken? "Are you here rather than at home because of Bobby?" I asked. "I mean, your home must bring back a lot of memories."

"Nah. Don't go making a big psychological deal. The wife did that. I'm here because I like it. I don't dislike the apartment I live in. It's a good place. Got a good deal on it for that neighborhood. If I owned that building, which I might yet, I could turn *it* over in a couple of years and make plenty. Nah, there's nothing wrong with that place." He finished the Scotch, glanced down toward his lower desk drawer, but left his hands on the table.

I stood up. So Felcher's home was not a home but a potential investment. How much of his life would he be willing to turn over for a profit? Was that what had happened to his wife? His son?

"Let me see your plans for the temple land again," I said.

Felcher hesitated, apparently struggling between caution and pride. Pride won. He extracted the architect's rendering.

It was the same giant box, with the same iron railings simulating balconies. No "form follows function" here. I looked at the windows, with the lines suggesting plants in the upper floors. And the lower floor—on its storefront window the tiny letters said "Self-Over."

"Kleinfeld's moving in on the ground floor?" I asked.

"Yeah."

"Isn't that a bit premature?"

"His money's as good as anyone's." Felcher reached down and extricated the Scotch bottle.

"How did you two come to arrange this?"

"I mentioned it. He said it was a better location than where he is now. We settled." He poured the Scotch.

"Do you put all your potential lessees on the architect's sketch?"

Felcher slammed the bottle back into the drawer. "Look, lady, I needed something down there. What do you *want* me to put in the windows—Joe and Mildred Scott, Harry Lumpkin?" He half drained his glass. "You got something I got to answer or not?"

"Not now."

Chapter 10

Self-Over was dark. I thought I heard footsteps inside. I knocked, waited. The footsteps stopped. I knocked louder. Still no response. Felcher had had plenty of time to call and warn his colleague. I didn't want to give Kleinfeld all night to perfect his story.

I circled to the alley beside the building. Two metal garbage cans blocked the entrance. I slithered between them and the wall. Leaves and papers littered the cement and garden snails crunched under my feet. I moved slowly to the rear, aware that my presence was obvious to anyone who was interested. I had radioed in my destination, but Kleinfeld didn't know that. The alley held for me the fear it would for any cop: I could be cornered—by Kleinfeld, by another of the suspects, by one of Berkeley's many crazies who just felt like offing a cop.

I checked behind me, then climbed the steps to the back door and knocked. Inside, in a room beyond, a light went off; I heard footsteps, first clearly, then growing softer, as though someone was moving toward the front door.

Jumping from the step, I ran down the alley, crushing more snails, pushing past the waste cans to the street.

Kleinfeld's door was shutting. Outside it was a woman in jeans and a hooded ski parka. Was she the married woman

Kleinfeld had mentioned? I hesitated.

The woman crossed the sidewalk and climbed into a yellow Triumph.

Making my choice, I remained in the shadows and noted her license plate.

When she pulled away, I walked back to the door and pounded.

It was several minutes and three more poundings before Garrett Kleinfeld opened the door. "It's after eleven o'clock," he said.

"It was earlier when I started knocking." I stepped in.

"Couldn't this wait till morning? I've had a rather long day."

"I can see."

He glanced toward the door.

I started to ask if she was the married woman of his alibi but decided not to. No need to tip him; I'd ask *her* that as soon as the Department of Motor Vehicles traced her. "What exactly is your relationship with Vernon Felcher?"

Kleinfeld sank down into a squat, arms wrapping around his back. "I told you, Bobby was a student—"

"The truth, Mr. Kleinfeld. Bobby may well have been a student of yours. Felcher may even have felt it helped him, but Vernon Felcher wouldn't be giving you studio space because he thought you were good for Bobby. Now, why is it that you will have the first floor of Felcher's building?"

Kleinfeld let his rump fall to the floor. His legs spread forward.

"Why?" I insisted.

Forgoing a new pose, he said, "It's because of our common feelings about Padmasvana and his crew."

"With that as a basis, Felcher could have filled the building."

"Let me finish."

"Okay." I squatted across from him.

"Because of our common dislike of them, when I discovered that Rexford Braga was having financial problems, I tipped off Felcher and he made an offer for the land."

"How'd you hear that?"

"On the Avenue. Surely you know how much makes the rounds on Telegraph."

Kleinfeld could be telling the truth. Among the sizable group of merchants, Berkeley's street artisans, students and hangers-on, a lot of information was disseminated. "And so, in gratitude, Felcher gave you the first floor?"

Now Kleinfeld bent one leg toward his body and twisted his torso away from it. "No, not free," he forced out. "I'll be paying for that space. But before you ask, I won't be paying as much as someone else would. I *am* getting that consideration. And, again before you ask, it's not because Vern Felcher is so filled with gratitude; it's because that's what I demanded from him in return for the information."

Catching his eye, I said, "And that, I suppose, is an example of operating to the fullest of your potential?"

The lines of his face tightened. He released his pose and turned to face me. "Yes, Jill, it is. What I teach here is very important, in many cases vital. It is the difference between letting an old car rust in the driveway and getting it overhauled. And there's nothing to say that I shouldn't use my knowledge to remove a danger to the community while at the same time providing a more appealing place for my students."

I glanced at my watch. I wanted to get back for the end of Pereira's session with Braga and his books. Time for one more question. "You know Felcher as well as most?"

"Yes."

"And you knew Bobby."

"True."

"Do you think Felcher cared much about Bobby?"

Kleinfeld bent his knee and pulled his foot toward his groin. "In his own way."

"Which was?"

Kleinfeld began to twist to the left.

"Look," I said, "I'm quite willing to wait you out. I'm getting paid for *my* time."

He sighed, straightening his leg. "Okay. What I'd say is, Felcher did not reach his potential with Bobby."

"In layman's terms."

Kleinfeld started to respond, caught himself and appeared to change verbal gears. "While he was married, Felcher didn't have much of a relationship with the boy. Then came the Felchers' divorce and the boy went to live with his mother in the Valley. She couldn't handle him, either— or so Felcher said. Felcher said she was soft. His standards are not mine. But, coming from him, that was not a compliment. Felcher brought the boy back here. He did try to get him into something constructive. Bobby was his only son, his heir. To a man like Felcher, that means a lot."

"Enough to kill for?"

"Of course. They let his son die. Now they're denying him the property. I wouldn't want to guess which is the greater affront."

"What do you know about that property?"

"You'd be surprised what I know, like that new law Berkeley has about multiple dwellings—the height limit?"

"Yes."

"Well, somehow Felcher managed to get a variance for that property."

"Hmm." So Felcher not only stood to make a killing on

the ashram property, but if he didn't make it there, that was it. He wouldn't get another variance. If anything, the zoning laws in Berkeley were becoming stiffer. The city council was definitely in favor of single-family dwellings.

"When you lose your child," Kleinfeld said, "and then latch on to something, and then the same people threaten to take that away, it could throw you over the edge."

Interesting, I thought as I stood up. Whatever Felcher and Kleinfeld's business relations, it certainly didn't extend to protecting each other from the police. Obviously, Felcher hadn't bothered to call to warn Kleinfeld I might be coming. He would have had plenty of time to eject his guest before my arrival. And Kleinfeld, for his part, was painting a good background for Felcher as the murderer.

And as I drove back to the temple, I wondered how much the new space meant to Kleinfeld. It appeared his following was dwindling. Certainly his afternoon class was nowhere near the size needed to support him. And Kleinfeld was ambitious, in a sense—rather like a younger, brighter, much more appealing Braga. Doubtless, he envisaged himself running a nationwide Self-Over, and the new location was an important step. The appearance of prosperity was vital to the appearance of legitimacy.

I got out of the car. The temple looked empty, the courtyard dark. Pereira would be downstairs in Braga's office poring over the books, asking Braga questions he didn't want to hear. I wished I'd reminded Pereira to keep someone at the door. Braga himself might not be a direct threat, but Chupada didn't fill me with confidence, and the Penlops—their combined juvenile record was longer than I wanted to contemplate.

I quickened my pace as I crossed the courtyard. Even the ashram was dark. My footsteps and the scraping of the jacaranda trees against the temple wall were the only sounds.

The basement door was locked but, as before, that presented no problem. The room beyond was dark, too. No light switch protruded from the wall. No light came from under the stage. The room was black except for the thin slice of light from Braga's door.

The residue of wariness I had felt in the alley beside Self-Over hung on as I moved toward the door. No voices were audible. I started to call out to Pereira, but stopped, careful to make my footsteps softer.

Stacks of tea boxes loomed.

I reached for the doorknob. Behind me there was a sound.

I stopped, looked around. Nothing moved in the darkness.

I turned the knob, opened the door. The room was empty.

I sighed, smiling at my melodramatic caution. So Pereira had finished quickly. And she'd unnerved Braga sufficiently that he'd forgotten to lock his door.

Was there anything else he'd forgotten? Should I take a look around, as long as—The lights in the room went out. I started to turn, reaching for my automatic. "Hold it!" I yelled. But the footsteps came quickly. Then a deeper darkness descended as the cylinder hit my skull.

Chapter 11

The phone was ringing. My head hurt. Vaguely, I knew I was lying on a cement floor and Nat was calling, demanding his Cost Plus stainless. Why was he calling now? Why couldn't he buy his own stainless?

I shook my head. It seemed to rattle. The phone stopped. I looked around. I was on Braga's office floor. My head throbbed.

Slowly I pushed myself up. I wished I could see my watch, but my eyes refused to focus. The light was on. Why was the light on now? How much time had passed? Was my assailant still here? I doubted that. But the possibility made me jumpy.

Reaching for the phone, I told the operator to get me the police station.

By the time the backup crew arrived, we searched the temple, I dictated my report on the incident, it was well after midnight. I realized I'd never been unconscious before, and although the time between the blow and the phone's ringing had seemed long, it couldn't have been more than a few minutes. But that was all I realized. I had no clue as to who my assailant had been. Anyone living at the ashram could have seen me and followed me to Braga's office. Kleinfeld could have followed me from his studio, Felcher from Comfort Realty. Or someone else might have been in the basement when I ar-

146

rived. They may not even have realized whom they were hitting. Whoever it was, it was someone who didn't want to be seen there, probably someone as interested in Braga's financial records as I was.

Shift had ended nearly two hours ago, but at the station Howard and Pereira were waiting, Howard sitting on my desk, his long legs extending out into the aisle, his shirt wrinkled, and a spot I remembered from yesterday still evident on its front. Pereira, blond hair curled and in place, uniform still starched, paced—partly from concern and partly from the tension of waiting to tell of her interview with Braga.

"I think," she said, as I finished explaining the lump on my head, "that Mr. Braga was unprepared for us. To begin with, I got to him just before two promising-looking marks were making their way along the receiving line after that big ceremony this evening. Then I asked for the books. He hemmed a little, but—now this is just a guess, of course—he decided I wasn't much of a threat."

Howard and I laughed. Connie Pereira, with her suburban-housewife look, had caught a number of suspects off guard. In fact, Connie had rarely even visited the suburbs. She had grown up in Oakland, the oldest child of an alcoholic father. Her mother had been in and out of institutions that offered the only respite available for the poor. Connie Pereira's goal was to get herself and her two brothers on a sound financial basis. What there was to know about money—accounting, bookkeeping, stocks and bonds—she knew, but she never had enough money left over from helping her brothers and bailing out her parents to try out her knowledge. Professionally, however, she made it come in handy.

"And were you a threat?" Howard asked her.

"Better believe it. It seems what Braga's books say is that above his own 'modest' two-thousand-dollar-a-month salary, the net is fifteen hundred. And what Braga says is that that amount is what the monastery in Bhutan demanded in exchange for Padmasvana."

"Hmm."

Pereira paced next to the desk. "Braga gave me this big song and dance about how he made more in his previous important position in L.A., which—I'll spare you his circumlocution—was doing PR for a bunch of unknowns in the entertainment field. He said he gave that up to devote himself to Padmasvana because he was so distressed at the shallowness of his life—no, wait! It gets better. So Braga signs on with Padmasvana to bring enlightenment—"

"Obviously not enlightenment to L.A."

"True. And now, with Padma's death, the temple will have to stumble along with Chupa-da until Braga can get the monastery to turn loose another guru, and"—she forestalled our comments—"that will be somewhat difficult for Mr. Braga because he says he doesn't know the name of the monastery. He says Chupa-da handles all the correspondence. The best he could do was to give me this piece of paper with what he thought was the name of the place, in Bhutanese."

I glanced at it. "We'll have to check it with the Indian Consulate. What'd Braga say about Preston, the baby, being the next guru?"

"He laughed."

"What'd you think of his story?"

"About the same as he thought of Preston."

Howard stood up. "You might also be interested in my findings about the temple and Garrett Kleinfeld's operation. My suggestion is that we retire to some quiet place where our beaten colleague"—he glanced at the bruise on my forehead—"can relax. Like her place."

My head still ached, but the prospect of having it ache at

home over a beer was appealing. "Sure, Howard. Connie, you know where it is."

"Yeah, but I have to call back Walden at LAPD. He said he'd give me the dope on Braga when he got back from assignment." She glanced at her watch. "That should be in ten minutes."

"Good, that'll give me time to check my in box and shovel out the mess at home."

"I guess, then, it would be a show of wisdom for me to come with Connie," Howard said. "You are okay to drive, aren't you, Jill?"

"Yeah. It's just a little headache now. More humiliating than painful." But Howard's concern was nice. Maybe I had been overly suspicious about his interest in my case. I picked up the papers from my box, glancing through them, putting a couple in the out box with okays, putting most back in the in box to consider tomorrow, and tossing one, a message to call Nat, in the waste can. On my way out I left the license number of Kleinfeld's woman friend with the clerk, to be called into the DMV first thing in the morning.

By the time I got home, my head felt like the snails I'd crushed in Kleinfeld's alley. I took three aspirins and looked around the room in amazement. I didn't think I'd been home enough to create *this*. Picking up my sleeping bag, I began to stuff the day's clutter into the closet, wash up the dishes that had been in the sink the night before and clear off room on the table for our drinks. No wonder Howard's wrinkled, spotted clothes appealed to me. I sympathized with Nat—for a finicky person, living with me must have been torture.

Still, if he could see this, he'd know why I couldn't find the Cost Plus stainless. Strange, I thought, as I straightened a pile of books on the floor, when we were deciding on the divorce, the end of our marriage had been devastating and now, not a year later, it had come to this triviality. Maybe the stainless was symbolic of more. Maybe I was too involved in the murder to see. Maybe it was best to keep it trivial. Maybe . . . But Howard and Pereira were at the door.

Howard held out a six-pack as he entered. As I took three glasses from the drain board, Pereira sat down and glanced around in silence. She had been here before, when I had first moved in. I had the feeling that she would like to have been able to say something nice about what I'd done with the apartment.

What she did say, "I caught Walden just as he was leaving. They had to drag him back from the parking lot. It took a while. That's why we were so long getting here."

My apartment must have been messier than even I'd realized. It hadn't occurred to me that they were late.

Howard took a swallow of beer. "Always good."

I nodded.

Pereira said, "According to Walden, Braga was known to the cops around the Strip. Seems he was something of a small time promoter, always hanging around kids who were trying to break into the business."

"Not impressive, but hardly illegal," I said.

"No. But Braga was marginally connected with a few payola rings. There was never proof but over a five-year period there were three complaints from kids he handled."

"Three complaints isn't that much." Howard took a healthy swallow of beer.

"That's what I thought," Pereira said, "but according to Walden, people in the business, particularly green kids, don't like to make police reports. And the last thing a kid wants to do is turn in the person who might help him make it."

"But payola's a way of life there, Connie. I can't imagine

anyone complaining—not when they're just starting out," I said.

Pereira leaned back. "The complaints were about skimming over and above the payola." Noticing our questioning expressions, she added, "The kids felt that Braga was taking an extra cut for himself."

"Like the monastery in Bhutan."

"Exactly, Jill."

"What happened to the complaints?" Howard asked.

"Dropped. Suddenly the complainants would have nothing to do with the police."

"A touch of the heavy hand from Braga?" I asked.

"Probably. To LAPD, Braga was a small-time nuisance, one of hundreds. 'A mere pimple amid the warts of LA. crime,' to quote Walden."

I took a drink to wash down Walden's observation. "So Braga was scraping by in L.A. Probably things were getting thinner and thinner. Braga's no fool. He must have realized that sooner or later there would be a kid he couldn't intimidate and he'd end up in court. So while he's pondering, he comes across Bhutanese Buddhism and somehow finds Padmasvana and brings him to this country and success is just around the corner."

"But after all those years in the entertainment industry, thinking in terms of stars and star managers, would being Padmasvana's assistant be enough?" Howard asked.

"Padmasvana's associate," I corrected him.

"Semantics."

"It's not like Braga eschews the limelight. When I was there with Ginny, it looked like the Braga and Padmasvana Show."

"Even so, you're talking about an audience of a couple of hundred. Let me give you ladies an insight into the male ego." Howard tilted back in his chair. "Every man has a certain vision of himself as President of the United States or the equivalent in his field. Like I see myself as chief —I know you see yourself as chief, too, Jill, but let's not get into it, because *I'm* going to be chief."

I raised an eyebrow. It hurt my forehead.

"Anyway," he continued, "as a man gets older, the vision tarnishes and there comes a point when he's middle-aged, and if he's going to hang on to that vision, if he's going to vindicate his existence, he needs one big success. For me, that one big success would be being chief, It would not be being public-relations officer. For Braga, I think it would be more than controlling an audience of several hundred."

"But Padmasvana's movement could have grown. It could have become as big as Transcendental Meditation," I said.

"Not without Padmasvana," Pereira said.

"And so," I went on, "when Rexford Braga hears that Padmasvana is planning to 'go,' he decides that he'll be more useful if he dies in a splashy way."

We sat a moment. Pereira finished her beer, glanced at Howard's, which was two-thirds down, and opened another can. My own glass was still half-full. I sipped thoughtfully. "The thing is, Braga's not the only middle-aged man with an ego to solve. What about Felcher, waiting to build his apartment house on the site of the temple? Or Kleinfeld? He's not so old, but he's got a lot of ego tied up in Self-Over. And with Padmasvana in the picture, his students were in danger of being co-opted."

"Speaking of Kleinfeld," Howard said, "you might be interested in what I've discovered about his finances."

"Yes?"

"Well, it seems that Mr. Kleinfeld isn't a total altruist, either. As a matter of fact, there's a good deal of similarity between the finances of the temple and the Kleinfeld operation. They both put a lot of pressure on their followers. You know the temple wants converts to give over all their possessions— a lucrative setup if they had a better class of convert. They encourage older people, and when they get them, they really press tithing—I guess that's the best they can do. You remember what Felcher told you about the old girl who willed them the property. Of course, she had so much money that leaving them the land may have been tithe for her. Still, Braga and company didn't waste time. They've been here for what? Three years? And who knows how many more wills they're waiting for?"

Pereira set down her glass. "So what's Kleinfeld's racket?"

Howard leaned farther back, balancing on the rear legs of the chair. "The Body-Over and other cute-named come-on classes are five bucks for a two-hour session."

"That's no fortune," I said.

"True, though at one point he had over a hundred students a week. But the thing he does for big money is Self-Over itself—a three-month course where he pretty much takes over the lives of the students: morning classes before work, a diet of vegetarian meals, evening classes, all-day seminars on weekends. For this, students pay in advance—fifteen hundred dollars. About two-and-a-half years ago, before Padmasvana became well known here, Self-Over had a wave of popularity. At one point, Kleinfeld had forty students in it at a time."

"Whew!" Pereira and I said together.

"And for an additional five hundred bucks, the students can come back to group raps or private sessions with the master himself forever. This is what keeps them untarnished."

I finished my beer. Recalling Kleinfeld as he talked about

his new studio in Felcher's building, I wondered if he was the type to kill to protect his establishment. Then I cautioned myself to forget that. "Types" didn't hold up in police work. Guilty types turned up innocent with appalling frequency, and Milquetoasts murdered without regret.

I looked from Pereira to Howard. They both sat caught up in their own thoughts.

Finally, Pereira said, "I know what's in store for *me* tomorrow—hours in the library with that symbol on the knife—but, Jill, where do you go from here?"

"Back to the temple, I guess. I think it's about time Mr. Braga explained in concrete detail just how he came upon Padmasvana."

Pereira nodded, picked up her bag and started out. But Howard stopped at the door. "You sure you're okay, Jill? That bruise looks like a ripe mango."

"Yeah, it's just . . ."

He moved closer, looking down at the spot, brushing my hair back from my forehead. "Sure?"

I hesitated. "I'm okay. Thanks."

He rested a hand on my shoulder, giving it a squeeze, then followed Pereira's path outside.

Chapter 12

Friday morning: a mere forty-eight hours from Lt. Davis's deadline for finding Padmasvana's killer. I washed down my aspirins with coffee then checked with the station. They'd got word back from the Department of Motor Vehicles Kleinfeld's visitor was one Katherine Mary Dawes, with an address off Telegraph.

It was already late. If I changed into uniform now, I could squeeze in the interview before shift began at three. That was presuming Katherine Mary Dawes was at home waiting to be interviewed.

But of course she wasn't. Her address was a large faded post-Victorian, remodeled several times and now used as a commune of sorts. There were plenty of them in Berkeley, some with political, some with religious, some with merely economic focuses. But they had features in common: they were places where messages, once left, were rarely received, and where police were not welcome guests.

"Where is Katherine Dawes?" I repeated patiently to the evasive, stringy-haired blond woman at the door.

She stared down at her moccasins. "She's not here."

"So you said."

"I'll tell her you were here."

"I'm sure you will."

She moved back, and when I took a step forward she didn't object, though her face wrinkled in wariness.

"You don't mind if I come in, do you?" I asked as I stepped into the littered hallway. To my left was a table nearly buried under old newspapers and letters. I wondered how many people were living here.

"Listen," I said. "I'm just trying to get some information from Katherine. She's really incidental to what I'm looking for. It'll save me a lot of time if you tell me where she is."

The woman glanced down the hall, as if trying to decide whether to seek reinforcement.

Before she could do that, I said, "It's a matter of time till I find her. I can have this house watched. I can run a Social Security check and see where she works. You're not accomplishing anything by making it difficult."

"Well, I—"

"Look, you know the officers on the Avenue, don't you?"

She nodded.

"Have they ever hassled you?"

"Well, no—"

"Or anyone else on this beat?"

"No, but the Health Department ordered—"

"I'm not talking about other agencies, just the police. We've been straight with people on this beat, and we expect the same in return."

She ran her teeth over her lip. At the end of the hall, the kitchen door opened slightly, sending forth an aroma that suggested fried mud.

"Okay. Kitty works at the Assessor's Office, in Oakland."

I almost laughed.

"If she takes the bus she should be home about five-thirty, right?"

"Yeah, if she's coming straight home tonight. Sometimes she has classes."

At least if she went to a class I had a good idea where to find her. Now I still had time before the staff meeting. If I moved fast, maybe I could catch Braga off guard.

He was in his office, head lowered over his books when I came in.

"Is there something we missed, Mr. Braga?"

He spun around in the swivel chair. If he was trying to disguise his displeasure, the effort was fruitless.

I sat on the edge of the desk, looking down at him. "We got a report on you from the police in Los Angeles. Seems you had rather an unsavory reputation there."

Pushing himself up, he paced to the middle of the small office and stopped. "I've never been arrested."

"Not quite, but almost—three times." I repeated the complaints Walden had told Pereira about. Braga listened silently, staring at the bruise on my forehead.

"All right, I'll admit I've made mistakes. Before I discovered Buddhism, I led an impure life. I did use people; I was competitive; I couldn't go with the flow."

I sighed. I would have preferred almost any other role. I had had the party line coming out of my ears. But there was no sense wasting time on that. I asked, "Just how did you come in contact with Padmasvana?"

"Do you mind if I have a cigarette? People are so *fussy* about smoke all of a sudden. Of course, I realize that smoking is an unhealthy habit, and I try not to do it in front of the Penlops, so the times I can smoke are severely limited."

I nodded, "About Padmasvana?"

He brought the match to the cigarette, puffed, blew it out. "Well, the way it was, Officer, was that I was in L.A. I'd gotten interested in Buddhism, like I told you, and one night when I was expecting nothing out of the ordinary, I went to a lecture given by a holy man from India. It was a small affair. There must have been no more than thirty people there, mostly young people.

"You see, Officer, young people are much freer, more willing to take a chance . . ."

"Less set in their ways?" My sarcasm was evident.

Braga stared, then continued. "This man was in Los Angeles just for a few days. He talked of well, I don't quite remember what his topic was, but he impressed me as very devout and knowledgeable."

I realized my finger was tapping against the desk. I stopped.

"He talked for maybe an hour, and at the end of that time he mentioned that he had come from a meeting with a young guru in Bhuta who was destined to be much greater than he." Braga waited till he caught my eye. "That young man was Padmasvana."

"And so you went to Bhutan?"

"No, no, Officer. Although I was deeply concerned with bringing such a leader to the spiritually thirsting young people of America, it was not propitious for me to travel to Bhutan at that time."

"Low on cash?"

He directed his reply to the loftier region above my head. "I wrote to the monastery."

"I thought you didn't even know how to pronounce the name of the place."

"I wrote through the good offices of the holy man in Los Angeles. He did the actual writing, in Bhutanese."

"Do you have a carbon of that?"

Braga laughed, the genuineness of his expression cutting

through his facade. "You don't save carbons of letters to Bhutanese lamas."

"Did they answer?"

"Yes, very rapidly. They said that an oracle had told them that Padmasvana was destined to bring the message to the West. As soon as I could raise the money they would be glad to ship to secure passage for him."

"And did you?"

Braga nodded. "It took me some months, but I did without, limited my intake to rice and vegetables, spent my free time reading spiritual books rather than going to movies and shows, and soon I had the money and sent it to the monastery. In a month Padma was here."

I pulled out my pad. "What was the holy man's name?"

Braga stubbed out his cigarette. "I'd like to help you, Officer, but I just don't remember. It was an Indian name, and I've run across so many since that *I* have no idea about his."

"What organization gave the lecture?"

"It was in a backyard in Van Nuys. I think I found out about it from a flyer."

"Okay, okay. So what happened when Padmasvana got here?"

"We started the temple. Of course, it was more modest than this. That was before Padma had a following. But we've found Berkeley to be a most receptive climate for Padmasvana's message."

I could imagine. Berkeley and the surrounding East Bay area had accepted the Black Panthers and the John Birch Society, the Symbionese Liberation Army and scores of lesser-known radicals. There were gay men's rap groups, lesbian mothers' groups and Baptist churches of all shades. The only place more open to fringe groups was L.A. Interesting that Braga hadn't tried there.

Footsteps sounded on the basement steps. Without thinking, I poised my hand over my holster.

Braga smiled, savoring my discomfort. I followed his gaze to the door where two Penlops had stationed themselves.

Obviously, the knowledge of my presence had spread quickly through the complex.

I turned back to Braga. "What about the tea? How much do you make from that?"

He was still smiling. "Very little. It is our service to the community. But do feel free to check that again, like your colleagues did last year when the unfortunate Penlop passed from us. Here"—he flourished a tea label—"it's packaged by Ho-Sun Teas in Chinatown. Thirty-one Drinnon Alley."

"I'll do that, Mr. Braga."

As I pushed past them, the Penlops looked questioningly at Braga but made no attempt to stop me. In the basement room, I looked again at the cartons of tea that lined the walls. Surely Braga couldn't be using them for anything so obvious as smuggling—smuggling from San Francisco, yet!

But then, Braga was no master of subtlety. Unfortunately, not subtle wasn't synonymous with dangerous.

Equally, unfortunately, it was now nearly four. Even speeding, I couldn't catch the end-of-shift meeting. And Lt. Davis wasn't likely to consider that Braga's information made up for my oversight.

I hurried up the steps and across the courtyard toward my car and almost smacked into Heather Lee and Preston.

She wore what from a distance could have been taken for a Penlop robe—a full-length brick-red garment tied with a bright cord. But up close the resemblance vanished. Heather's robe was silk. Whereas the Penlop garments hung loose, Heather's was fitted and featured a very unPenlopian plunging neckline.

I hesitated, then decided arriving at the station at four-thirty was not much worse than four. "It looks like you're taking the role of regent seriously," I said.

Heather boosted the baby up, ignoring my comment.

"Preston is Padmasvana's child, isn't he?"

When she still didn't answer, I moved to her side and looked at the child. He had olive skin, a round face and Padmasvana's eyes. In Bhutan, he might not have been distinguishable as Padmasvana's son, but here, with the suspects for paternity limited, there was little question. "That's why you were so angry when Chupa-da moved into Padmasvana's room, isn't it? That's why you said Preston had more right to be there."

Shifting the child to her other arm, she said, "Yeah, okay. I didn't want it to be public knowledge yet, but it has to come out eventually. This is Padma's son, his heir, and the rightful person to follow in his footsteps. And if Chupa-da thinks he can just step in and take over he has another thing coming. I'm not going to let this baby be done out of his inheritance." She strode back across the courtyard with me alongside.

"What do you plan to do?"

"I'm going to make sure Preston gets his proper place. I'm going to see that no ceremony goes on without his being there. I'm going to see that the Penlops understand who he is—and Braga too whether he likes it or not. I'm going to . . ." She had come to the ashram stairs. She paused momentarily, then, spotting Leah at the door, she bolted up the steps and deposited the baby in her arms. Noticing my ill-concealed skepticism, she said, "I'm *going* to do all those things. You think I don't care about Preston. But you're wrong, wrong. He's my child, and I care about him. It's just that tonight I have to go out."

"And miss the ceremony?"

"There isn't going to be any ceremony."

"But I thought there would be memorials for days. Are you sure, Heather?" The idea of Rexford Braga's missing an opportunity for another six hundred dollars was inconceivable.

"Of course I'm sure. Otherwise I wouldn't be rushing back to my tepee to get dressed, would I?" With that she began to hurry back to the tepee.

I followed. "Where are you going?"

"Tonight is the Chattanooga Charlie Spotts concert. Didn't you see the posters? Chattanooga's really far out."

Pushing back the flap of the tepee, she strode to the clothesline inside and extricated the sequined cowboy outfit. "I was afraid I wouldn't be able to make the concert. I was really bugged."

"You thought Leah wouldn't be able to watch the baby?"

"Nah. Why wouldn't she watch him? She likes that type of thing. She really gets off on picking up after people and being the big comforter. Besides, what else would she do? I mean, if she didn't have this place and all those pimply adolescents running around needing her, what would she do? She's lucky to have Preston to take care of. Someday when Preston is famous, when he's more famous that Padmasvana, she'll get a lot of points for having done a little something for him."

Heather slipped off the silk robe, revealing a silver lace bra and matching panties. She sat down at the dressing table and began rubbing cream on her body.

I had the feeling she'd almost forgotten I was there. "Heather," I said, "why does Braga bring in so much tea?"

She rubbed the cream on her thigh. "Who knows? Chupada gets the stuff. He rides off into the sunset in the Padma-bus."

The Padma-bus. I had seen the multicolored old VW van.

Somehow I hadn't considered Chupa-da, the monk, as a licensed driver. "Only Chupa-da goes?"

Heather finished the leg and began one arm. "Yeah, I think at the place where he buys it they only speak Chinese. Braga doesn't speak Chinese. He has a hard enough time in English." She laughed. "Besides, it's Chupa-da's thing. He thinks it's a big deal, driving to San Francisco."

"But what does the temple get out of the tea?"

Heather finished one arm and paused. "Jeez, Officer. The stuff's two dollars a box, you know. And twenty-four Penlops push it every day."

"And that's all?"

Heather shrugged and turned her attention to the remaining arm.

I considered insisting. The obvious move was to stroll across the courtyard and open a few of those cartons. But it was nearly five, getting dark. The wind was picking up and all signs pointed to the first heavy rain of the year. Katherine Dawes would be hurrying home from the Oakland Assessor's Office.

Chapter 13

I spent twenty minutes in the entryway at the commune under the nervous eye of the same hostess before Kitty Dawes appeared. When she arrived from work, she looked like a young woman from the middle economic stratum of the Bay Area. She had long brown hair, and wore a western shirt and jeans.

I introduced myself. "I need some information about Self-Over. I understand you're one of the students there."

She hesitated. Wariness appeared to fight with eagerness to proselytize. The latter won. "I was in the first Self-Over class. That was four years ago. It changed my life."

"How so?"

She led me up the sagging staircase, through an array of toys, paper bags and general clutter on the landing, to a surprisingly comfortable room at the end of the hall. I settled in an over-stuffed chair as she continued her tale of self-improvement, i.e., any situation can offer some thing for Number One. When she wound down, I said, "Are you still seeing Garrett?"

"Oh, yes. There's a continuing program. You can go back to support groups and you can even have private sessions with Garrett."

"And that's what you do?"

She beamed. "Yes. I meet with Garrett at least once a month."

"And do . . . ?"

"We talk about my progress. How I'm dealing with my life. How things are better. What opportunities there are that I should be aware of."

"Does Garrett meet with all the graduates so often?"

Her smile grew wider, and I felt sure I was on the right track. "I doubt it."

"You must be important to him. Maybe more than just a student."

"There's no such thing as 'just a student.' "

I nodded. Damn it, I was forgetting the lingo of the game. Now I'd have to spend time reassuring her. "Perhaps as one of the founding students, I mean . . ."

She smiled again.

"When did you last meet with Garrett?"

"Last night."

"And before that?"

"Let me see." She pulled a date book out of her purse. "You learn to keep records when you work in the assessor's office. Garrett says that's good. It keeps you from missing things. He says working in the assessor's office has been good for me. Ah, wait here. Last month, the twenty-third."

I stared. That was two weeks ago. "Not since then?"

"That's still more often than a lot of people see him."

I lowered my voice. "Kitty, it's important that you tell me the truth. If you were with Garrett and don't want people to know . . ."

"Hell, my old man wouldn't care, if that's what you mean. Garrett's not like another guy, you know. It's not like that. I'd tell you if I'd been there more. But you see, I'm handling my own problems now and I don't need to go so often. I usually go once a month, unless . . ."

"Unless?"

The door opened and a tall man in overalls walked in.

Kitty turned, relief evident on her face. "This is David," she said. "My old man."

"David Allbright," he said, extending a hand with a confidence and ease that seemed out of place in this building.

"We'll only be a couple of minutes," I said. "I was just asking Kitty about Self-Over."

"Oh, yeah." He flopped on the sofa next to Kitty. "Great thing, Self-Over. That's where Kitty and I met. Really been a big help to both of us, but particularly to Kitty. She still sees Garrett."

"You were going to tell me what you talked about, Kitty."

The look of wariness was back on her face. She stared at David, waiting for him to answer for her. I wondered what, indeed, Self-Over had done for her.

"Besides your personal growth," I insisted.

Still she hesitated. "Well, we talk about my job."

I started to remind her she'd already said that, then stopped. "What, specifically?"

"Well . . ."

"About the assessor's office? About taxes?"

"Well . . ."

"Go ahead, Kitty," David said. "There's nothing wrong with what you're doing."

"You won't tell my boss," Kitty pleaded. "I don't think they'd understand. There are funny little customs at the office."

"If it's not illegal, we don't tell anything unnecessary."

"You're sure?"

"Sure."

She pulled her feet up under her. "Okay. I have a special

arrangement with Garrett. You see, there's a list of properties with delinquent taxes. You probably know this. If your taxes are delinquent for five years, the property automatically reverts to the state."

I nodded.

"Two years before that there's a list published."

"Uh-huh."

"Well, at that time a lot of real-estate people read the list and buy up pieces cheap. Anyone can do it. Anyone can see any of our records any time. You could walk in there tomorrow and ask for records and see how long the taxes were overdue. It's easy to find out about a specific property. But it's not so easy to find out *all* the properties that are going to be on the delinquent list."

"So?"

"Don't you see?" All her hesitation was gone. "If someone doesn't pay taxes for three years, getting slapped with late charges all the time, there's a reason, and it's usually because they don't have the money. And they might be willing to sell the property below market value."

"And Garrett Kleinfeld wanted to know who those people were?"

"Yes. He had a deal with a realtor. I don't know how many they bought up. I forget. But it must have been quite a few."

"And what do you get out of this?"

Now she beamed again. "Before I went to Self-Over, I would have given Garrett the information just because I thought so much of him. But I've really learned to watch out for myself. Other people pay five hundred dollars for the group meetings and private sessions. Mine are free."

I stood up. "One last question. Did you tell Garrett about the Padmasvana temple property?"

She looked puzzled. "I don't know. I just have addresses,

and I see so many I never remember them."

It was well after six when I arrived at the station. I checked my desk, finding nothing new concerning the murder, signed a couple of forms and threw out the latest message from Nat. How long would he be willing to eat with his fingers in order to get the satisfaction of possessing the conjugal stainless? And come to think of it, why, after all these months, had he suddenly developed this passion for reclaiming it? That had not occurred to me before.

Banishing thoughts of domestic problems, I considered how to handle the thornier problem of having missed the staff meeting. Lt. Davis's office was down the hall. Many times I had approached it with considerable trepidation, but none more so than now. Its very tidiness made me uncomfortable. And the lieutenant had the habit of observing a case so closely that he found seventeen small but necessary things left undone. More than once I'd left that office feeling incompetent. But the cases did get done, swiftly.

Now I decided to give him the meat of the Kitty Dawes interview, and hope. "Lieutenant," I said as I sat on the hard chair, "it seems there is a long-standing business relationship between Garrett Kleinfeld and Vernon Felcher."

As I recounted what Kitty Dawes had told me, he sat back, fingering his mustache, eyes half closed, as if capturing the picture under those dusky lids.

When I had finished, he said, "And what do you conclude from this, Smith?"

"As far I know, it's legal and probably quite profitable. I'd suspect Kleinfeld is getting a bit more than reduced rent in Felcher's building."

"And?"

I had often wondered whether the lieutenant's proddings

were aimed at eliciting points that he himself had already discovered or whether they were in fact merely proddings. But I
pondered those sorts of thoughts at home. Now I rushed on
with the facts. "Three years . . . Well, one thing is that
Kleinfeld led me to believe that he knew Felcher because
Bobby came to some of his classes. Obviously, that's twisted
backward. He knew Felcher a good year before that."

"And?"

"And"—I leaned forward—"that's probably why Bobby
went to Self-Over. Maybe he was a conduit between
Kleinfeld and Felcher."

"Why would they need a conduit? Their arrangement is
not illegal."

I sat back. "True. A bit melodramatic. No reason they
couldn't just phone one another." I stared at the pile of papers at the corner of his desk, so neatly stacked, no errant
edge presuming over the line. "But still, Self-Over doesn't
seem like something that would appeal to Felcher. He's not
likely to pay hundreds of dollars for a philosophy that he
could explain to his son in half an hour. And even the introductory classes—the ones Bobby went to—aren't cheap. I
can't believe that was all just for Bobby's benefit."

"Why, then?"

"That I don't know. If Felcher had Bobby going to Self-
Over for a reason, what reason? The boy had been living in
Visalia with his mother. Felcher brought him back here and
sent him to Self-Over. Why?"

The lieutenant tapped his finger on the edge of the desk.
"Try a different tack. What actually happened then? You understand?"

"Uh-huh. Well, a Penlop came along and recruited
Bobby, and—Oh, okay. So Felcher and Kleinfeld set Bobby
up to be recruited and live in the ashram so that . . . so that,

well, so that he could keep an eye on their potential investment."

Lt. Davis's finger stopped. "Or so he could do something
that would ensure their getting the land."

"Or find out something."

"And maybe he did." Our words were coming faster.

"And Padma's people learned about it and killed him."

For a moment we both sat silent, bemused by the way our
ideas had suddenly clicked into place.

It was the lieutenant who spoke next. "Okay, Smith, try
that. Young Felcher finds out something damaging in the
temple, and in order to keep him from reporting back to
Felcher Senior, someone there kills him. Hmm. Yet and still,
the question is, what could he have found out that would have
been so incriminating?"

"I'm not sure, but if the ashram was a potential investment
turned up by Kitty Dawes Kleinfeld-Felcher, that would
mean it, unlike her religious institutions, was not exempt on
property taxes. That seems an expensive oversight on Braga's
part."

"In order to qualify for a religious exemption," the lieutenant said, "a church must prove to the Investigators from
the assessor's office not only that it is nonprofit, but also
that the church building is used solely for religious pur-
poses."

"Ah. So the tea business could disqualify them. It must be
bringing in a bundle."

"Hmm. Or the threat of financial investigation is the deterrent."

I stood up. "Whichever it was, if we think the temple crew
killed Bobby Felcher, that idea must also have occurred to
Felcher and Kleinfeld. It certainly gives Felcher a class-A
motive for doing in the guru."

The lieutenant nodded. "Check it out, Smith." I started for the door.

"And Smith, be here for staff meeting tomorrow—on time."

Chapter 14

I drove quickly to Comfort Reality, but for once the office was empty. Had Kitty warned Kleinfeld, and had Kleinfeld broken with tradition and warned Felcher? Or had Kitty even bothered?

I called into the station. The man on the beat checked Felcher's home address. Nobody there, either. I sat in the car, watching the traffic, thinking. The rain had started. The streets shone, and to the eye of a cop, looked lethal. It hadn't rained since March. Now, a mere six months later, it was as if drivers had forgotten everything connected with slippery roads. Either they were cutting in and out of lanes or inching along in first gear. Before the night was over, the department would be jumping. I was glad I was no longer on traffic detail.

I sat back, picturing Lt. Davis at his desk, staring at me, the ever-present finger smoothing his mustache. "If you can't find Felcher, then what else do you need to know?" he would be asking me. What else? What else? What was it that Bobby Felcher had found out?

The obvious move was to drive across town and have a look at those tea cartons.

I started the car.

It took a quarter of an hour to get there. Though the rain slowed driving, it had the advantage of keeping people off the

streets and, more important now, out of the temple courtyard. For once, as I headed to the back of the temple, there
was not a Penlop in sight. The rain was already soaking into
my wool uniform, and I hated to think how I'd smell, much
less feel, in a few minutes. I reached to try the knob of the
basement door.

In the rain I almost missed the sound of voices coming
from Braga's office window.

Releasing the knob, I moved closer, the water dripping
down the side of my hat as I listened.

"You think you can get more for this land, Braga, you
try." I recognized Vern Felcher's voice. From the clicking
that underlined his phrases, I could picture him playing
nervously with one of his ballpoint pens. The footsteps I
took to be Braga's habitual pacing. For nerves, they were a
real pair.

"Nobody else will buy this land," Felcher went on. "Get
that through your head."

"We'll see." Braga's simulated calm contrasted with
Felcher's clipped delivery.

"Nobody else will *want* it. Listen, how long did the old girl
you inherited it from own it—thirty years? Maybe even
longer, right? You know what termites can do in thirty years?
You know how much dry rot you got here? You see those
cracks? I can tell you what that says about your foundation.
Listen, what you got here is a temporary dwelling. Look at the
angle of this floor. You put a marble on it, it would crash
through the wall. You're talking about jacking up the struc-
ture and sliding in a new foundation. You're talking twenty
thousand bucks, just for the temple. Then the altar boys'
house, that's an even bigger job. Nobody's going to buy a
wreck like this place."

There was silence broken only by the slap of Braga's feet

and the clicks from the ballpoint pen. The rain splatted on my shoulders.

"I know about your variance for the land." Braga, using his professional voice, still sounded uneasy. "Don't try to cheat me, Felcher."

"It's not worth a hundred and fifty now." I could almost see Felcher's leer of victory. "When you had a going concern here, maybe, but now—Listen, Braga, you better get out while you can still make a profit. Another month and all you'll have here will be a wayward boys' home."

"Now that's where you're mistaken. You're looking at the ashram only on a materialistic plane."

Felcher snorted.

"No, no. In another month I will have a new guru straight from the monastery in Bhutan. He will meet his followers under the memorial statue of Padmasvana."

"Where you going to get the dough for that? I know your habits, Braga. In another month the state'll sell this place for taxes."

"The faithful will be anxious to contribute to the memorial. They'll empty their pockets in one last show of love."

Felcher snorted louder. "You got ten days. In ten days you can have a hundred and twenty thou in your pocket, or you can be standing here empty-handed, waiting for the termites to finish off this place. You got ten days, Braga."

The pen stopped clicking. Footsteps moved away from me, toward the office door. Neither man spoke.

The footsteps stopped. "Braga." Felcher's voice sounded assured. "Maybe you don't want to sell this place. Maybe you want to let those guys from L.A. come up here and beat their hundred thou out of you, huh? Yeah, I know about that. And those boys don't like to hear 'no.' "

"Forget it, Felcher. I've got time."

"Time, hah! What—a month, two months, with 'interest' piling up? There's no other way for you to get the dough, and the longer you wait, the worse off you are."

I expected Braga to protest, but he didn't. I would like to have heard his rebuttal. For Braga, those physical threats added the stick to Felcher's hundred-and-twenty-thousand-dollar carrot and explained why he would kill Padma now.

I hurried around to the front of the temple in time to catch Felcher. "I need to know the details of both your offers for this property."

Felcher stared. "The offers? Offers are private matters." Oddly, he ignored my eavesdropping.

"Nothing's private in a murder investigation."

Felcher's fingers pressed together hard, as if he missed his ballpoint pen. "I never wrote out an offer."

"Come on, Mr. Felcher. You offered Braga some amount. How much?"

He moved in toward me till the curve of his paunch nearly brushed me. "Lady"—his voice was softer—"I got my affairs to protect. I can't have this getting around."

I nodded.

"Look, it's like this. I gotta have this parcel in ten days or my variance runs out. I hadda work like hell to get that, and there's no chance of them coming up with an extension on it. But Braga don't need to know that. The point is that what the parcel would have brought a couple of days ago—"

"I heard your reasoning when you explained it to Braga," I said sharply. "Look, Mr. Felcher, what you and Braga have here is a conspiracy to defraud the rest of Padmasvana's organization. Now, I'm—"

"What? I'm not conspiring. I'm just buying land—and the title's in Braga's name. I got a lawyer. Believe me, when this goes through it'll be legal. All my part will be strictly on the up-and-up. I don't give a shit what Braga does then."

"That may be, Mr. Felcher. But I suspect if word of this should get out, say, to the papers or the city council or any number of other places, it could throw a monkey wrench into your plans."

"Is that a threat?"

"Tell me about your offers."

"Okay, okay. Before, it was a hundred and fifty thou. Now it's a hundred and twenty. Okay? Go arrest speeders."

"Not so fast. You think he'll take it?"

"You didn't hear him say no, did you?"

"He didn't say yes, either."

"He'll take it. He just wants to push for more, but more he ain't getting. He'll drag it out till the last minute; then he'll take it."

"And . . ."

"Look, lady, it's pouring, in case you hadn't noticed. I'm no duck."

"Okay, my car's here." I opened the door, and reluctantly, he got in. When I'd opened my own side, I said, "What did Bobby find out about the temple?"

"What?"

"I know about you, Kleinfeld and the assessor's office. And I know you planted Bobby here."

For the first time, Felcher seemed to deflate. He sunk back into the corner of the seat. "And they killed him, the bastards."

"How can you be sure?"

"They said he overdosed."

"Mr. Felcher." I softened my voice. "The autopsy showed he overdosed. His record wasn't exactly clean."

Felcher sat up. "Clean, hell. So the kid took pills—plenty of pills, I'll admit that. But that's all he took. And then all of a sudden he overdoses on heroin."

"I know it's hard to live with a child's death. But when a kid's used to one type of drug, experimenting with another isn't unusual."

Felcher stared blindly out the window. The rain smacked against the windshield. Headlights made long slippery patterns on the street. "Look, lady, there was no way that kid would have shot up that heroin. No way. He was terrified of needles."

"Maybe he'd outgrown that."

"In six months, not likely. Look, I was gonna take the kid overseas. A trip to Hong Kong. The kid wanted to go. He coulda impressed his friends, he woulda gotten a free ride. He really wanted to go. But he didn't. You know why? Because he needed shots to go, that's why. He turned down a free trip rather than get those shots."

"So then you've suspected all along that Bobby was murdered." It backed up the lieutenant's and my speculations.

"Yeah, yeah. You're thinking this gives me an even better motive. Maybe. But I'll tell you, I never needed more motive. Believe me, I coulda killed the lot of them."

"Mr. Felcher," I said, "what was it that Bobby found out about the temple?"

Felcher shook his head. "I wish I knew. I can't tell you, lady, how much I wish I knew. But if he discovered whatever they're hiding, they got to him before he could tell me."

Braga was at his desk when I looked in the door a few minutes later, his stiff hair hanging on slumped shoulders. Another time, I would have felt almost sorry for the man.

I stepped inside. "I heard what you said to Felcher. I've just talked to him, so you'd better be straight with me—and quick."

Braga turned in his chair, then started to get up. His white shirt was wrinkled, and circles of sweat underlined each armpit. "So you heard? What more can I say? I owe a hundred thou to men who aren't going to wait. You want me to tell you about the gambling? The threats?"

"No. I want to know what Bobby Felcher found out about the temple or that tea business when he was here."

"Listen, Officer—"

"No, you listen. What did he find out? I don't want to have to ask again."

Involuntarily, Braga moved back. "Bobby was spying, was he? Of course, he would be."

"Come on, Braga. You're not that dumb."

Braga pushed himself up from his chair, looking straight across the desk at me. "I will not be intimidated. We have nothing to hide here. If Bobby was searching for evil here, he was doing so fruitlessly."

"Okay, then let me see the tea boxes."

"The what?"

I strode out to the basement room. The brightly wrapped tea boxes were stacked against every available foot of wall on both side walls and the back, in piles four feet high. Braga followed me; his steps, which had once had a firmness of authority on stage, were now labored. Why was he dawdling? What difference would a few seconds make?

The back door opened and two large Penlops entered. Now Braga stood straighter.

I looked directly at the Penlops. One was like all the others I'd seen—bleary eyed, slow moving. But the other, the blond Penlop who had spoken to Leah deVeau the day I'd met her, had a hint of life in his eyes, a look of skepticism. I wondered why he was involved with the temple. And I wondered which of the two would be more dangerous.

The light glittered off the cellophane wrappers of the tea boxes, giving the odd illusion that the Ho-Sun yellow dragons were dancing against their blue-and-red backgrounds. With all those tiny boxes it was like looking through a kaleidoscope.

Taking a breath, I turned back to Braga. "The tea boxes?"

"Very well, Officer. Here." He walked toward the back wall. "Shall we start here?"

"No, I'll take one from this side." I moved to the wall opposite the office door.

Braga hesitated, then nodded. The Penlops stepped behind me.

"Move them back," I demanded. "I don't need them breathing on my shoulders."

Braga signaled the red-robed boys with a tight movement of his head. They backed off. Braga stood straighter. He reached for one of the top boxes, but I shook my head and grabbed one near the bottom, balancing the boxes above it precariously as I pulled it free.

"I presume the police department is going to pay for this," Braga said.

"Bill us."

The cardboard top pulled out easily. I removed one of the bags and sniffed. It smelled like tea. Was there nothing but tea here? Hard as it was to imagine the tea as a cover for smuggling, it was even more difficult to think that it served no purpose at all. I moved to the other end of the wall and pointed to a box in the middle.

Braga hesitated again, then followed and pulled out the box.

It, too, held nothing but tea.

By the office door, the Penlops stood, hands hidden in the pouches of their robes.

I turned toward that wall, glancing up and down the rows of boxes.

"Officer, how many are you going to open? This is taking time." Braga's voice was choppy.

"As many as I need to. You'll get paid for them; you shouldn't care. It'll save the boys the effort of selling them. Start here." I pointed to one midway down the third row from the corner.

Braga extricated it and opened it. Just tea.

I indicated another nearer the office door. It, too, held only tea. I tried one near the bottom of the row by the door, one midway up on the opposite side of the office, one nearer the back door. More tea.

"Officer," Braga said triumphantly, "this is merely wasting time."

"We'll see." I stepped back. There had to be something here. I squatted down, running my eyes slowly, carefully, up one row and down the other, looking for something different about one group of boxes.

"Officer, I have to insist."

The Penlops took a step in my direction.

I continued examining the rows, checking the Chinese characters, the bright blue, red and yellow on the wrappers, looking for cellophane that had been opened and re-sealed.

"Officer, if you want to continue this, you'll have to get a warrant."

"Here!" I pointed to the bottom of the row, three from the office door. Stepping forward, I pulled it out. It looked like four boxes of tea; the wrappers were like all the others. But it was one box, a metal strongbox, covered in tea wrappers carefully taped down to look like four boxes side by side.

Braga grabbed it and thrust it into the hands of the blond Penlop.

"Mr. Braga—"

"No. It's private."

"Nothing's private in a murder investigation." I seemed to be voicing that concept frequently today.

Braga stepped between me and the box. "Mr. Braga, I insist on seeing that box."

"No." His hands were pressed against his thighs.

"Do I have to get a warrant?"

He said nothing. His face was white, his lips pressed tightly together.

"Very well, I can get a warrant. It's a waste of time, but—" I headed for the phone in Braga's office. The blond Penlop edged toward the back door.

"Come here!" I said. "You and that box stay in my sight till the warrant gets here."

He stopped, looking not at me but at Braga.

Braga seemed to be considering his options.

"Get him back in here," I demanded.

Braga hesitated, then nodded, and the Penlop stepped away from the door.

I went to the phone and dialed the station. "This is Smith. Give me Lt. Davis," I told the clerk.

"He's in conference," she said. "But Pereira's left a message that you should talk to her the minute you called or came in."

"Okay. Put me through to her first." From where I stood I could see Braga and the blond Penlop. Their eyes were not contacting one another. Braga appeared caught up in thought. The Penlop looked alert and wary.

"Jill?"

"Yes, Connie."

181

"Listen, something really big has happened with the case. How fast can you get in here?"

"What?"

"There's no point in talking about it on the phone. Whatever you're doing, it's not as important as this."

"Listen, I need a warrant to open a strongbox here at the temple. I can't leave until I get it."

"Jill, I'm not exaggerating. Nothing in that box could be as important as this."

"Then tell me!"

"Jill . . ."

I made a quick decision. "Okay. Get the warrant procedure going for me. Send a couple of men down here to relieve me, and I'll be there as soon as I can. But your news had better be as big as you say it is."

"Believe me, Jill, it is."

Chapter 15

The backup men arrived in fifteen minutes. The warrant would take much longer.

I drove as quickly as I dared across town. The rain was coming down hard and steadily. The accidents I had foreseen earlier were now realities. Crinkled bumpers and dented fenders marked the busier intersections, and pulsar lights from patrol cars seemed to slide along the wet streets around them.

When I arrived at the station, the squad room was resounding with the insistent ringing of phones.

"Wait," Pereira said into the receiver as I approached. "She's just arrived. Put them on hold." She beckoned me to hurry. "You've got two calls on hold. One from your husband."

"Ex-husband," I said mechanically.

"Whatever. And one from an Elizabeth deVeau."

"Okay. Thanks, sort of. But what about this big breakthrough that's so urgent?"

"Piqued your interest, huh?" Pereira grinned. "I'll get us some coffee while you take your calls. The deVeau woman's on line three, your ex-husband on two."

"Okay." I looked at the two blinking lights on the phone. What could Leah deVeau want? I started to punch line two, for Nat, then stopped. No, I *knew* what he wanted.

I pushed line three.

"This is Officer Smith."

"This is Leah deVeau, dear. I wanted to talk to you about what's going to happen here. The boys are getting edgy, having their future so unsettled. Of course, I've tried to assure them that the temple will go on as before and that everything will be normal as soon as Mr. Braga gets the successor from Bhutan, but you know how boys are. And these boys have had years of bad experiences, and with the police here all the time—"

"Leah." I interrupted the spurt of words. Her call was clearly not urgent and I was anxious to hear Pereira's big news. "Are you sure your concern is merely for the boys?"

"I am *very* concerned about them. No one has ever questioned that." She sounded indignant.

"I'm sure you are. But what about yourself? Aren't you a bit concerned for your own future?" Line number two continued to flash.

"Well, yes, I am," she conceded, a little reluctantly. "You know, I've never had a job before. And I *am* good at this. It makes me feel there's some purpose to my life. It's important to me." She paused. The light on the phone flashed. Its badgering annoyed me, as if Nat were sitting there tapping his finger, as impatient with me as I was with Leah. "It's *very* important," Leah went on. "You see, here I'm a success. I do something that matters. In the cosmic scheme of things, I'd say I do something considerably more important than the president of General Motors, for instance."

Pereira set down the paper cups, then settled back in the chair across the aisle, making a show of twiddling her thumbs. Nat blinked on line two.

"Well, Leah, if there were anything definite I could tell

you, I would. I know this is vital to all of you. But you shouldn't have to wait too much longer."

"But—"

"I'm sorry. There really is nothing more I can say." My tone was harsher than I'd intended, and Leah's "I'm sorry; goodbye, then," sounded small and distant.

A wave of guilt engulfed me as I put down the phone and took a breath, but by the time I pushed line two, the guilt had turned to anger.

"Look, Nat, I'm in the middle of a murder case. I don't have time to deal with the stainless. You've lived for months without it, but I'll gladly send you twenty dollars—which is about what we paid for the stuff—if I can have the pleasure of your not hounding me for it."

In response, the dial tone hummed in my ear. I put down the receiver.

"He'd already hung up," I said sheepishly. "Maybe it was just as well."

Pereira shrugged. She'd heard enough of my complaints when I first separated from Nat.

"So what's the big news that's more important than the sealed box waiting for me at the temple?"

She took a swallow of coffee, drawing a huffed fingernail across the paper cup. Then she leaned forward.

"I will spare you the details of my trip to the Indian Consulate, but when I talked to the man who knows about Bhutan and who was interested in Padmasvana's being killed, he'd already notified the authorities in Bhutan. And guess what?"

"What?"

"There's no record of Padmasvana leaving Bhutan and entering the United States."

"But—"

"And"—she'd raised her voice to cover my interruption—

"they checked and found there is no such monastery and no such town."

"What?"

"Yeah."

"Well, what was written on that paper Braga gave us?"

"Nothing. Just Sanskrit letters. They weren't even words. The guy I talked to said they looked like someone had been practicing writing the letters—like an exercise tablet."

"Was he sure? Couldn't it have been some strange dialect?"

"I asked him that. He said no. There are eight major dialects in Bhutan"—I nodded, for that confirmed what Braga had told me—"but Bhutan is really a small country as far as population goes and not that many of the inhabitants are literate, so that the written word there is pretty easy to know—if you're an Indian official. The address Braga gave us is more like a sheet of paper where someone hit the keys of a typewriter randomly."

"But that doesn't mean the monastery didn't exist."

"That's what I told the guy. But he said no, that if there were a monastery that had sent a guru to the United States in response to Braga's request, they would have located it by now. And remember, Padmasvana left no immigration records in either country."

I leaned back against the desk, staring incredulously at Pereira. Finally I said, "If there was no Padmasvana from no monastery in Bhutan, then who have we got in the morgue?"

Chapter 16

Suddenly a lot of things became clear. What we had here was a racket—a phony pretending he was a guru. No wonder people had not heard of Padmasvana before he started the temple in Berkeley. No wonder the money Braga had said was going to the nonexistent monastery in Bhutan exactly matched what was left over after the temple deducted its expenses.

I remembered my search of Padmasvana's cell. I had noticed his English-Bhutanese dictionary. I had assumed he was a Bhutanese trying to learn English. But, indeed, he had been an American looking for a few Bhutanese phrases.

The more I thought about it, the clearer the whole scheme was. It was so simple. Padmasvana stood on the stage and mouthed nonsense syllables. How many people spoke Bhutanese?

In Berkeley, there were people who had been to India, people who had studied Tibetan at Buddhist centers, Indian students at the university. Braga had been clever enough to steer clear of anything connected with those countries. But, as Pereira's research had confirmed, Bhutan was an isolated country in the Himalayas, one that was too mountainous for all but the hardiest of tourists, one that did not draw Americans.

Also according to Pereira, the Bhutanese people lived in valleys separated by mountains nearly as tall as Everest. That was why, though they numbered only about a million, they spoke in eight major dialects. So when Padmasvana (or whatever his real name was) had made his pronouncements, tossing a legitimate Bhutanese word here and there amid nonsense syllables, even a person familiar with one section of Bhutan would have assumed he spoke the dialect of a different area.

I recalled Padmasvana, his eyes that seemed to look directly at me, his compassion, his warmth. I had been taken in right along with everyone else.

Still, knowing the man was a fraud didn't tell us why he was murdered.

To Pereira, I said, "I want to see each of the suspects separately. Scout up where they are and then keep an eye on Braga when I'm done with him."

She nodded and, leaving word with the dispatcher, we headed for the temple.

"Who was he, Braga?" I demanded.

The Penlops had been taken upstairs. Braga stood at his office door and stared over my head. I could imagine the weighing of alternatives going on. Finally, with a sigh, he said, "Paul Lee."

"Paul Lee?"

"Yeah. I chose him for his face. He was perfect for the part. Goddamned kid, why the hell couldn't he just go along and play out his role? I could have gotten Orientals in L.A. who could have done the job, and they would have understood what they were doing. Dammit! I should have known better than to take on an amateur."

"Where did you find him?"

188

"Seattle. He was a student. He worked part-time in a Chinese restaurant."

Suddenly, I began to laugh. It was all so ludicrous. Pulling myself together, I asked, "And Chupa-da?"

"Paul's brother. Joe."

"Was he a waiter, too?"

"No. Goddamned kid, why'd he have to go and get himself killed?"

"That's what I was about to ask you."

Braga glared.

"Before he was killed, that night, he said, 'I will go.' What did he mean?"

"I don't know."

"Think." I settled atop the desk as he began pacing the small room. "You're in a lot of trouble. I wouldn't want to consider the number of laws you've broken or the civil suits you'll be open to. Your best move is to be as cooperative as you can, about everything I ask you." He stopped, and I said, "You understand that, don't you, Mr. Braga?"

"Yeah," he said disgustedly.

"About this 'I will go'?"

"The damned kid was planning to leave. He would have done it months ago, but I kept babying him along, telling him about his responsibility to the Penlops and the rest of us. It would work for a while, and then he'd decide he wanted to leave again. Every goddamn week I'd have to spend an hour or two hours or sometimes a whole goddamn night going at him. He was like a spoiled kid, like some goddamn teenager who just wants to split."

"Why? Why did he want to go?"

He threw up his hands. "Who knows. He always was a quiet kid. Maybe he was bored, maybe he wanted a piece of ass, who knows?" He looked directly at me. "What more can a nineteen-year-old kid want than to be guru to hundreds of people? Jesus!"

I slid off the desk. "It seems to me, Mr. Braga, that you are a lot better off with him dead than with having him leave."

I had expected outrage, but Braga merely nodded. "Yeah, it didn't take me long to figure that out."

"It'll go easier if you confess, you know."

Now I got the outrage. Braga's face reddened, his hands knotted to fists. "Listen, lady, I been straight with you. I'll admit that the kid was a pain in the ass, but I didn't kill him." He grabbed my arm. "I could have jollied him along for a couple of weeks more, maybe a month or two. I could have gotten another kid, a professional, to replace him. I could have told the house that he'd been called back to Bhutan and some new kid had been sent to be guru. I didn't have to kill him."

"Braga didn't have any choice." Joe Lee, a.k.a. Chupa-da, sat in the desk chair under the skylight in his attic room. He'd already tried to dissociate himself from Padmasvana. He'd come from a different monastery; he'd only met Padmasvana over here; he'd had his suspicions about him. A discussion of birth certificates, fingerprints and Braga's statement brought the change.

He had flopped in the chair and said, in unaccented English, "Damn!"

"What do you mean, Braga didn't have any choice?"

"Braga's a fool, but he's not a moron. He didn't understand Paul. He didn't bother to try. But even if he had tried, I don't know if it could be done. Paul was a dreamer, a soft kid. He was the baby. He always had things easy. I mean, there he was in college. He didn't work as hard as I did, but I never got to go to college. I graduated from high school and got this job pushing papers in an office downtown. Their token Chinese. But Paul, no, that wasn't good enough for him. My parents gave him the money they'd saved. They decided he was the bright one, the one who should have the college education. He was the one who would carry the family name to success. He was the one they gave all the opportunities. And then they told me I should help him!"

"You could have said no."

"It's useless trying to talk to you white people! You're all alike. You know nothing about Chinese culture. Look, in a Chinese family you don't say you're not going to help educate your brother. It's your duty. You say you're not going to help, and you're disgraced. The whole community looks at you like you're a leper."

"Okay, so you helped your brother through school. He had a job, didn't he?"

"Yeah, so he worked a little. Big deal. So he had a boring job a few hours a week for a few months. My job was forty hours a week for forever."

"I think we're getting off the track. You were explaining why Rexford Braga had no choice but to kill him."

"Yes, well, you can see how spoiled Paul was. He didn't plan any of this. Braga and I did all the spadework. Paul didn't bother learning about Buddhism. I had to dredge up all the doctrine. Wouldn't you know it—the one thing my family could have been useful for, and they had to be Methodists!" He glanced at me and, getting no encouragement, said, "Everything went fine for a while. We set up headquarters three years ago, and within a month we had followers and money."

I sat down on the daybed.

"Then Braga came up with the tea thing. We didn't make a fortune on it, but it kept the Penlops out of our hair. Before that, the damned kids were underfoot all day, demanding to be taught, to pray and to be blessed every time we turned around. With the tea job, they were out on the streets by eight and good and tired when they got back."

In any case, I thought, they'd doubtless made enough to cover the loss of not being tax-exempt. I asked, "Didn't anyone from Seattle or the college ever turn up and recognize Paul?"

"No. I guess we were lucky. I touched up the pictures, changed his hair, added the Buddhist robes. But still, it could have been a problem." He stood up, his embroidered robe hanging from his shoulders. "Paul, though, he didn't worry. All this time he never bothered himself with any of the problems. He didn't do any of the work here. Then suddenly he starts to get interested in Buddhism. I could see it coming. It was like the time he got hooked on spacemen when he was a kid. All of a sudden he was spending all his time in his room reading about Buddhism. He was going around being a guru—not just pretending, but really getting into it. And then he decides he wants the real thing. He wants to go away to a real monastery and be a real monk. He wants to just up and go!"

"And?"

"And? I talked to him. Braga talked to him. We kept him under control for a while, but I knew Paul. He was a spoiled kid. If he wanted to go, sooner or later he'd go."

"So why didn't you just let him?"

"I told Braga that. I told him I could take over. After all, I was the one who knew the stuff. But no, Braga wanted Paul's face. I told him about Paul." Leaning forward, he said, "The thing with Paul was that you could never trust him. Paul was like a child. He could have agreed to go away and let Braga bring in a replacement, but there was nothing to say that a month from now he wouldn't decide that wasn't ethical. Then he would have blown the whistle. Braga could never have been sure."

"Nor could you."

He froze, then shook his head slowly. "There's no point in talking. You'll never understand Chinese families. A Chinese man does not kill his brother."

"You seem Westernized enough."

Chapter 17

"It took you forever to find out." Heather sat in the tepee, brushing her long sandy hair. It floated from the bristles of the brush onto the shoulders of her beige lace negligee. The lacy gown-and-robe set was the type of thing I, as a teenager, had assumed I would wear on my twenty-first birthday. As Heather did now, I'd sit in front of a makeup table in the leisurely hours of the morning (though it was now 10:30 p.m.) and dab my fingers into the bottles that would make me instantly beautiful. Somehow, for me, that state of adulthood had never arrived. Now, at nearly thirty, not only did I not have a makeup table or a lacy negligee, I didn't even have a bed.

Turning my mind back to Heather's smug observation, I said, "You could have told me."

"Why?"

"Heather, this isn't a game. Padmasvana—Paul—is dead."

She didn't reply.

"When did you find out he wasn't a Bhutanese?"

She glanced at the various garments hanging from the clothesline next to her. "A long time ago."

"When?"

Pulling out a long ruffled skirt, she held the material across her chest and looked appraisingly in the mirror. "I don't remember exactly." She picked up a plastic container, unscrewed the top and wiped her finger across the red paste in it. With precise strokes, she formed a triangle on one cheek, then the other.

"When was it in relation to the time you met Paul Lee?"

She smoothed in the color and held up the skirt again, smiling.

"Heather!" I grabbed her shoulder and spun her around. "Put the skirt down and pay attention!" I waited while she pursed her lips, considered and then, with a scowl, obeyed. "Now, tell me exactly what happened when you met Paul Lee and how you came to find out about him."

"I suppose this means there's not going to be anything for Preston." Her scowl deepened. "It's not fair! It isn't! Look at all I've done, and now he'll get nothing. It's Paul's fault, damn him!"

"When did you find out about the hoax?"

"About six months before Preston was born."

"And what did you do?"

"Hell, what should I have done? Had an abortion?"

"What *did* you do?"

"I told them—both of them—that they better take care of me and my baby. They owed me that."

"And then you moved in?"

Heather shook her head. "They said it wouldn't look right. Prigs. I wasn't about to get some crummy room in some dive. I told them. I told them good, and they believed me. So they let me use the yard."

"And you set up your tepee?"

"Yeah."

"Heather," I said, realizing the question I was about to ask had no bearing on the case, "how did you come to have a tepee?"

"What? Oh, I bought it at school. I was thinking about becoming a Native American Studies major."

"Did you?"

"No. There was too much weird stuff. I never got around to declaring a real major. I was thinking about Bus. Ad."

The thought of Heather studying business administration temporarily silenced me. In the pause that followed, Heather stood up, dropped the robe to the floor and pulled her nightgown over her head. She replaced it with a striped caftan and grabbed for the hairbrush.

As she brushed, I said, "Paul Lee said he was 'going.' What did you think about that?"

"Lee was a bastard!"

I waited.

"A selfish bastard. How could he think about going off and leaving me and Preston here? What would that leave for Preston? I told him what a rotten louse he was."

"And how did he react?"

"Like a bastard. He gave me some gobbledy-gook about a higher way. Something he had to do. Some garbage about how he had to make things right. That he felt responsible because that Penlop overdosed. He was full of it. You know what happened to him? I'll tell you. I took this acting class in school. I played this character, like Camille, only it wasn't Camille. But the character was sick. She coughed. She was always weak. And after I did it for a couple of weeks, I really thought I was sick. You see?"

"You mean Paul Lee got carried away and really thought he was a guru?"

"Yeah. He got swell-headed. He didn't care about anyone. He just wanted to do what he wanted to do. He didn't even give Preston a thought."

"So what did you do when you realized he planned to leave?"

"I told you. I yelled at him." She was yelling at me.

"What—besides telling him what a bastard he was—did you say?"

"When he said he didn't care about Preston, I told him I would expose him. But he laughed. He said it didn't matter; something about him already being exposed where it counted. He said I could do what I wanted, but making a fuss would only disrupt the setup here. I told him I was going to do it, anyway."

"But you didn't, did you?"

"Chup-da—Joe—told me not to. It would only have hurt Preston."

It would have removed any chance that Heather, Preston or Joe could cash in.

"Did you believe Paul wouldn't tell anyone later?"

"I don't know. The crummy bastard. He probably would have."

"So what are you going to do now, Heather?"

"Now? I'm just going to live here in my tepee and take care of my child. Maybe I'll see Chattanooga Charlie Spotts again. I saw him last night; I really turned him on."

I stood up. "Well, don't leave Berkeley without talking to me, not with Chattanooga Charlie or anyone else."

Heather peered into her mirror. "Don't worry, I'll take care of myself."

Doubtless she would, I thought, as I made my way across the courtyard to the ashram. I was pretty sure I would find Leah deVeau somewhere inside, taking care of Preston. For all Heather's sureness about the future, I doubted she would find another setup like this, with her room and board taken care of, her position as consort and her on-call baby-sitter.

I looked through the house, finding Leah neither on the porch nor in her room. When I pushed open the kitchen door, she jumped and planted herself protectively in front of the stove.

"Oh, it's just you," she said. "I was afraid it might be Mr. Braga or Chupa-da or one of the Senior Penlops." She turned around and resumed stirring the pot on the burner. In the corner, asleep in a wicker basket, lay Preston.

I moved closer to the stove, drawn by the hearty aroma.

"Beef stew," she whispered. "I'm making it for tomorrow. Mr. Braga would be furious. Chupa-da would be scandalized. We're supposed to be vegetarians, you know."

"Surely Rexford Braga doesn't care that much about points of doctrine?"

"No, I don't think so." She held out the spoon for me to taste. It needed salt. "What Mr. Braga would really object to is the price of beef. He seems to think that all there is to nutrition is being full. Really, dear, if I—"

"Leah," I said, "I know Padmasvana was a fraud."

She nodded.

"You knew that?"

"Oh, yes."

"Is that why you called me this afternoon? To find out if I knew?"

"Partly."

"You could have told me." When she didn't reply, I asked, "When did you find out?"

She moved the wooden spoon around in the pot. "I really couldn't say when. Living here with Padmasvana so near, I saw him do things other people didn't see. He wasn't as careful about being 'on' here, if you know what I mean."

"What types of things did he do?"

"Oh, nothing big. It was just that sometimes I'd see him sitting listening to the Penlops talk. But I could tell that he wasn't just listening to sounds like you would if someone was speaking in a foreign language. Sometimes when they'd say something peculiar, like teenagers do, he'd almost laugh. And little things"—she smiled—"like carefully rolling up the end of the toothpaste tube, or squirming when he had to sit cross-legged for a long time. Or . . . I can't think of any more specifics, but you see what I mean—things a Westerner would do that a person from a rural Eastern country wouldn't."

"But there must have been a time when the full realization hit you."

She shook her head. "There might have been a time when it could have, but you see, it really didn't matter. I told you, I'm not much interested in doctrine. Frankly, I think you believe whatever you want to believe and you have as much chance of attaining nirvana as anyone else. I've been so busy taking care of the boys and you—" She turned to coo at the sleeping baby. "The doctrine, it was just gift wrapping. Inside of the box, it's still the same. It'll go on being the same."

"I doubt that."

"Oh, no. It has to go on. This is a good place for these boys. They'd be on the streets otherwise, into drugs."

"This place hasn't always been drug-free," I commented, and was immediately sorry I'd mentioned it. Leah drew back, and the expression of hurt couldn't have been more real had she been at the ashram during the time Bobby Felcher had lived here.

"There are no drugs here now," she said firmly. "I see to that. I take care of these boys. This is my place—watching out for these boys. Their parents don't have to wonder about them here. Nothing's going to happen to them."

I decided not to pry loose Leah's certainty about the future. She'd know soon enough that the ashram would have to be closed. Instead, I mentioned Paul Lee's words at the last ceremony.

"He got very serious toward the end," she said. "He began to resemble a holy man. He looked less like one of the boys. In the beginning, I think he really cared about the boys. I don't know whether he would have left them. But he said he would, so I suppose he would have."

"Then what would have happened?"

"Just what's happened now. Mr. Braga would have gotten another guru. I thought for a while he'd promote Chupa-da. I never thought he'd wait around for Preston. Only Heather was *that* naive. But I did figure he'd move fast."

"But suppose Paul had exposed the fraud?"

"Oh, he wouldn't have done that."

The baby opened an eye, stretched, half whimpered and Leah picked him up, cooing at him again.

"Leah," I said, "if Paul Lee had exposed the operation here, if the whole operation had gone under, how much of a financial loss do you think that would have been for Rexford Braga?"

She concentrated a moment on adjusting the baby on her hip. "Honestly, I don't know. I don't think about finances above what it takes to feed and keep the boys. And I knew Padma would never have done anything like that."

I made no reply. Leah didn't want to hear anything negative about one of her boys. Up until now I had enjoyed talking to her. I had assumed her observations to be shrewd, but now I wondered how clear her vision was. I wondered if she saw the real world or one skewed to fit her wishes.

"Officer Smith." A rookie whose name I couldn't remember stood in the doorway.

"Yes."

"The warrant you wanted. It's here."

Chapter 18

I hurried across the courtyard, followed by the rookie—Olson was his name—and down the steps into the basement room.

There everything was as I'd left it. Braga was pacing, and despite the presence of the Penlops, he was smoking. Crushed butts lay on the floor like buoys marking his path. Beside the metal strongbox stood the backup men who had replaced me and, beside them, the two Penlops. The one with his eyes half closed was slumped back against the pile of tea boxes; the other, blond, alert, looked almost eager. I wondered how long it would be before word of Padmasvana's fraud spread to the Penlops. And, when Leah realized how thoroughly they had been used, what form their retribution would take.

I held out the warrant, but Braga shook his head. Silently, he extended a key. The blond Penlop holding the box stepped forward impatiently.

I took the box. It was light, much lighter than I'd expected. Could it be, after all this, empty?

The key turned easily. The Penlop leaned forward as I pulled up the top.

Inside was a sheet of paper, folded once. I lifted it gingerly, trying to touch only its edges and, much to the consternation of the blond Penlop, walked into Braga's office and shut the door.

I admit to killing Bobby Felcher. I let him have some downers, then I injected him with heroin so it would look like he had overdosed. I did it by myself. No one asked me to. I decided to do it because I found out Bobby had been watching me and saw me reading English and figured out that I was a fake.

It was dated six months ago and signed Paul Cheung Lee.

So Paul Lee had killed Bobby Felcher.

We would run the normal check on the note, of course . . . I replaced it in the box and called Rexford Braga in.

"How did you make Paul write this, if indeed it is Paul's writing?"

Braga slumped into his desk chair. "It's his writing. The paper must be covered with his fingerprints. They all saw him write it and put it in the strongbox—Joe and Heather and Leah. I called them together, had them watch, so Paul couldn't deny that note later. You ask them."

"Okay, I'm assuming it's real. How'd get you him to do it?"

"We struck a deal. I suspected Paul had killed Bobby. Paul wanted out. I wanted to be sure he wouldn't blow the whistle."

"How do I know you didn't first make him kill Bobby?"

Braga looked up, a genuine expression of amazement on his face. "Come on, Officer. If I couldn't convince Paul to stay here, in a perfect setup for a nineteen-year-old, do you really think I could have talked him into murder? I wish I had that much power." He let his head sag, not bothering to wait for my reaction.

Giving him the usual warning about not leaving the area, I walked out and headed for the station.

★ ★ ★ ★ ★

I glanced quickly through Pereira's reports in my in box, and caught Howard as he was leaving. Together we entered Lt. Davis's office.

I placed the strongbox on his desk. Pereira's report lay on the near corner. So the lieutenant already knew that Padmasvana was a fraud.

"Paul Lee killed Bobby Felcher. He gave him an overdose." I sat on one of the hard wooden chairs and recounted the whole series of interviews.

Carefully, lifting the confession note by one edge, Lt. Davis examined it. Finally he said, "So what have we got here?"

"First, Paul Lee killed Bobby," Howard said.

"But did anyone besides Braga know that?" the lieutenant asked.

"Heather, Joe and Leah—they saw him write the confession. And Paul, as Padmasvana, did say he was responsible for the death of the Penlop. He said it at several ceremonies. That would be enough to confirm anyone's suspicion."

"It gives Vernon Felcher a nearly peerless motive," Howard put in.

"And Kleinfeld, his partner?" the lieutenant prodded.

"I doubt it," I said. "Paul Lee's death didn't affect their dealings with Braga substantially. If Felcher killed him, it was mainly a personal vendetta."

The lieutenant rubbed two fingers over his mustache. "And the suspects at the temple?"

"I don't know," I said. "None of them would have killed Paul to avenge Bobby. On the contrary. If one of them murdered him, it had to be to prevent his leaving."

"Which, unless we've missed something, leaves us where we were before you found the box, Jill."

I stared at Howard, feeling as deflated as Braga had looked half an hour ago. "Yeah."

Lt. Davis sat back, his eyes half closed, his unspoken demand for thinking space dominating the room. "Let us speculate on what would have happened if the operation had been exposed."

"Braga'd have gone to jail," I said.

"And when he got out, he'd be a felon, an aging felon, with no chance of doing anything big again," Howard said. "He'd be lucky to pull off anything small, after that. Bad for the old male ego." He nodded knowingly at me.

"And dangerous if he couldn't pay his debts," I added.

"I think we've established sufficient motive for Braga," the lieutenant said.

I jotted down the names of the other suspects. "Okay, the ashram would fold. Leah deVeau would probably have to apply for welfare. She might get a foster-care license to keep children, but she'd have to have a place to do that in, and I don't know if she could swing it. In any case, she wouldn't be able to keep the same type of setup as she has at the ashram."

The lieutenant did not look impressed.

"Her position there is important to her. She seems to care a lot about the Penlops."

"Yet and still, Smith, it's not like having loan sharks at your throat."

I couldn't dismiss Leah's loss that way, but there seemed little point in pressing the issue. "Joe Lee would be in jail. He voiced a lot of resentment about his younger brother this afternoon—'My brother got everything.' I could see him getting into a rage at the idea of his brother undercutting the operation he helped set up."

"Particularly if he was planning on being the next guru," Howard said. There was no hint of a smile on his face now; it was all concentration. "Look, here's Joe Lee's choice—Paul blows the whistle and lands him in jail, or Paul dies and Joe becomes guru. There was no reason for him to suspect that he wouldn't make it as guru. For motive, that's got everything that Braga's does."

"Right. Who does that leave, Smith?" the lieutenant asked.

"Heather Lee, Paul's wife or mistress."

"What happens to her?"

"Well, right now I think she's hoping to take off with Chattanooga Charlie Spotts, the country singer. Before that she was planning on being regent till her baby became old enough to become guru."

Lt. Davis checked the sheet before him. "The child is not a year old. That's quite long-range planning."

"Plans aren't too clear in Heather's mind. If she wants something enough, it seems to her that she should have it. I'm sure she never considered the work or the politics involved in protecting the child's position for twenty years. She's only twenty years old herself."

"What I'm asking, Smith, is how she felt it would affect her future if Paul Lee revealed the fraud." His fingers began tapping.

I ran my tongue over my lower lip. It was hard to think of Heather having such clearly defined thoughts. Still, she knew how to look out for her interests. She had got Paul Lee to allow her to set up her tepee in the courtyard, where it had to have caused comment and potential dissension. She had maintained a position within the ashram community while apparently doing nothing to aid the movement. No, Heather was not the laid-back young woman she appeared.

"I'd say her motive was as good as Braga's," I said. "Either Paul keeps his role and she becomes Mother Divine, or he tells all and, if she avoids jail, she goes back home in disgrace, or she gets a job as a cocktail waitress and spends her off-hours changing diapers."

"Knowing about Paul Lee's fraud clears up very little," Lt. Davis said. "Well then, Smith, what about Garrett Kleinfeld and Vernon Felcher?"

"Felcher stands to save about thirty thousand dollars on the property now that Padmasvana's dead. And, of course, he is convinced someone in the temple murdered his son."

"Right," Lt. Davis said. "So much for his motive. What about Kleinfeld?"

"Kleinfeld. Well, knowing about the fraud might have given him material for blackmail or, more probably, he would just have turned in Braga and the crew. He has a pretty strong dislike for them. But he's under control. I can't see why he would have killed Padmasvana, and let . . ."

"Smith?"

"Well, lieutenant, there's something going on with Garrett Kleinfeld that I can't quite figure out." I took a breath, deciding what was the best way to phrase my suspicions. "At the time Paul Lee was murdered, Kleinfeld says he was with a married woman whose name he can't reveal."

"You haven't pressed him, Smith!" The lieutenant's fingers hit the desk.

"Well, no sir."

His fingers lifted and poised tight above the desk. "You think you *could* do that, Smith?"

"Yessir."

"What about the weapon?"

"Nothing new," I said. "It's a cheap knife. No chance of tracing it. As for the insignia, or whatever, on it—the markings that look like a box with lines extended down and to the right—Pereira couldn't find anything in the library. You've got her report. I've asked Braga and Joe Lee if it was some Bhutanese symbol, and they both said no."

"I think, Smith," the lieutenant said, making an ill-concealed effort to control his irritation, "that we can assume Braga and Joe Lee would have no more familiarity with a Bhutanese symbol than we would. No one connected with the temple would."

He was right. Was I losing my grip? Or was I merely tired after a grueling day? "Of course," I said, half to myself. "Now that we know the temple has no real link with either Bhutan or Buddhism, doesn't that make it even more likely that the markings are not a Bhutanese symbol?"

"Check it out yourself, Smith. You can start your day tomorrow with that."

Chapter 19

"Jesus Christ. I'm lucky to be still on the case, much less in charge." I glared at Howard, who was waiting in my desk chair, legs extended across the aisle. I'd spent the night—too worried to sleep—surrounded by questions that either defied solution or whose answers only increased my anxiety. Why hadn't I checked out the knife with real Buddhists in the first place? And when I learned Padmasvana was a phony, why hadn't I seen immediately that that raised more questions about the markings on the knife? And the whole temple fraud and Paul Lee's confession—what leads did they give me?

Now it was Saturday afternoon. Lt. Davis's Sunday deadline was closing in. The sleepless night had taken its toll; I felt like I was running on coffee alone.

I sat atop the desk, looking down at Howard.

"I didn't pressure Kleinfeld," I said. "Even a rookie would have."

"Jill—"

"I spend ages waiting for Berkeley's slowest judge to get off his duff and issue the warrant, and then the box gives us not a thing . . ."

"That's not exactly true, Jill."

I waved off his palliative. "And then there's the knife." I shoved the picture of *that* under his nose. "And who knows what, if anything, the scratchings on it mean?"

Howard pulled the picture from my hand. It had come within inches of his nose. He looked down, making a show of studying the photo.

I found myself staring at his expression, again wondering about his interest in my case. Nat, whom I had trusted, had lied, affirming a love that no longer existed for months before I had let myself realize it. And when I did, my cache of trust had dried to a hard lump. Now I begrudged parting with the tiniest portion of that lump. I demanded that my friends and colleagues repeatedly prove their honesty, integrity and loyalty. They were paying for Nat's betrayal. I knew that. But I couldn't stop doubting.

My attention had been pulled inward, but when I refocused I realized my eyes were still on Howard and he was staring back.

"You need any help?" he asked.

"Obviously I need all the help I can get."

"So what can I do?"

"You can give me any ideas you have on that symbol or whatever it is on the knife. Otherwise you know what's in store."

He grinned. "Yeah—interviews with every Buddhist in Berkeley, and Lt. Davis might waver and let you delegate that research to me. Okay." He stared down at the picture of the knife. "Suppose we assume for a moment that it is not a Buddhist symbol?"

"Suppose we do."

"It looks like a block drawing of a house, a Cape Cod house with the first-floor roof. What it looks like is a Chinese character representing a Cape Cod house."

"Howard!"

He tried, not very successfully, to swallow his grin. "Okay,

okay. I'm serious now. No Cape Cods." He continued to focus on the picture, his smile fading. His waves of red hair hung forward, nearly obscuring his face. "When I was a kid, I went through a period of marking things, put hearts on tree trunks, that sort of thing. I etched my initials on everything I owned and a good bit of stuff I didn't own. And one thing I learned—besides how angry my mother could get when I marked her silver bracelet with a big H—is that it's a lot easier to make block figures, particularly on something that looks as slippery as that knife."

"So you think they could be block letters?"

"I didn't say that." When I looked questioningly at him, he said, "But let me see. You have to allow for a little hand slippage. It could be *A 7*, if the second vertical line of the *A* doubles for the vertical line of the *7*."

I stared at the photo. "If that could be an *A*, it could also be a *P* or an *F* or even an *R*."

"Right."

"*A T, P T, F T*; or *R T*? That doesn't help much. The only way it could be initials would be if Padmasvana had had a last name beginning with or if Rexford Braga is really Rexford Braga."

"Or Fexford Braga. Or Pexford—"

Laughing, I said, "Enough. This is getting me nowhere."

"Okay, let me look again. *A T, P T,* or is it *A F?* Hey, what about *F?*"

"*A F, PF, FF, RF?* Hmm. Pity it's not *VF*. I don't suppose Vern Felcher has another name?"

He didn't have time to reply. The answer must have come to us simultaneously. *R F*—Robert Felcher. Bobby Felcher.

"Bobby Felcher's knife. Someone killed Paul Lee with Bobby Felcher's knife, Howard!"

"Which leads us right back to Vernon Felcher."

"Or Garrett Kleinfeld," I said. "And I have other things to find out from him."

"Oh, my God," Garrett Kleinfeld said. "I've seen that knife. Bobby Felcher's knife. Of course." His burst of candor was suspiciously sudden, but I decided to withhold comment.

"He had it here, during a class. He flashed it around. You see, Bobby wasn't any prize as far as stability went. He wasn't anywhere near in sufficient control of his own being—"

"About the knife."

Kleinfeld stared. Clearly, he wasn't used to being interrupted. "The knife. Well, as I said, Bobby waved it around. He obviously felt that since he was involved with his father and me he could get away with whatever he liked. I had to put a stop to that. So I told him firmly to put it away and take it home."

"And?"

Kleinfeld looked away. It was the first time I had noticed him deliberately avoiding my gaze. "He didn't. There was a scene. It disrupted the entire class. I told him to get out. He started to scream. Well, I screamed back, and . . ."

I controlled a smile. There was something amusing about the Self-Over guru's discomfort. "And?"

"Well, I came close to hitting him. He was furious, nearly out of control. He screamed, 'Home? I'll take it *home!*' and then he stalked out."

"And then?"

"Well, the class was a mess. I had to do a lot of intensive work with the students—"

"About Bobby . . ."

"That was a Friday. Bobby usually went to the Valley on the weekends, so by the time Felcher saw him on Monday he had calmed down. Felcher bought off whatever hurt feelings he had, and the kid was back here the next week, sulking, but here."

"And that was the last time you saw the knife?"

"Yeah. I guess Felcher must have made that point real clear to him."

"Do you know how Felcher bought him off?"

Kleinfeld shook his head. "No. That was between them."

"I guess I'll see Vern Felcher, then."

"Why?" Kleinfeld's hands tightened.

"You said Bobby took the knife home."

"Oh, yeah, sure. I guess you should see him." He looked hopefully toward the door.

"One more thing, Mr. Kleinfeld. The night of the murder, where were you?"

"I told you. I was with—"

"Names."

He looked at the floor thinking. "Okay, I guess I should have told you the truth."

"You *were* lying." This I didn't look forward to admitting to Lt. Davis.

"Yeah. There wasn't any woman."

"Then you were alone?"

"No."

"You were with a man?"

"It's not what you think." Kleinfeld looked truly abashed. Apparently, homosexuality was not something a fully realized person practiced. "I was in the Penlops' house."

Great. In proximity to the temple and the stage. Wonderful.

"I was there meeting Walt. You know, that big blond Penlop, the one who looks like he's still alive."

"Yes." The one who had been so eager to hand me the strongbox.

212

"He was giving us—Vern and me—information," Kleinfeld went on. "I mean, since Bobby died, we had no one inside. Walt was, well, keeping an eye on things. Or at least supposedly. He never really gave us much of anything. He just said stuff like 'Chupa-da bought more tea'; 'Braga looks nervous.' " Now the words tumbled out. "I told Felcher it was a waste of money, but he insisted we needed the protection in case anything unlikely happened. And it was his money, so, well, you see . . ."

"I do see." Catching his gaze, I repeated, "I do see." I gave him the same warning I'd given Braga and headed for the car. I called into the station and left word where I was going, then drove across the town to Comfort Realty.

"I don't got enough problems without you here again?" Felcher slammed his desk drawer shut.

Dispensing with the preliminaries, I pulled out the photo. "Do you recognize this?"

"The knife?"

"Yes."

He stared at it for almost a minute. "I suppose that must be the knife that killed Paddy-guru."

"Why do you say that?"

"Why else would you be showing it around?"

"Okay. But does it look familiar to you?"

"Hell, no. Listen, lady, what kind of dumbo do you take me for? You think if that were my knife and I'd used it to stab Paddy, I'd be telling you?"

"I didn't say it was yours. I—"

The phone rang. Felcher jumped for it. "Comfort Realty." He listened half a minute, his hand reaching for the ever-present ballpoint pen, then said angrily, "Don't give me that self-sacrificing crap again. Look, I'm in the middle of negotiating a deal, I don't have time . . ."

Where had I heard this before, I wondered as I watched him snap the ballpoint in and out?

"All right, all right. Half an hour." He slammed down the receiver.

"What was all that?"

"The laundry lost my shirt."

"Really?"

"What about the knife?"

"Never seen it."

"Mr. Felcher, that knife belonged to your son. It was Bobby's knife. His initials are scratched on it. I have a witness who remembers seeing him with it."

Felcher stared at the photo, then at me. "So what are you saying? You think Bobby rose from the grave, grabbed the knife and stabbed Paddy? You think there's some justice in the world, maybe?"

Ignoring that, I said, "Bobby said in front of several witnesses that he was going to take the knife home. He was living with you."

"Nice of Bobby to be so cozy in public. Home, huh? He never called it home. He never accepted my apartment as home, even though he had his own room. I worked sixty hours a week to make a place for that kid, and you think he'd call it home? He never . . ." His voice trailed off.

"The using wasn't one-sided. You did bring Bobby to Berkeley to have him infiltrate the temple. You set him up."

Felcher pressed his thumb against the already limp end of the pen. "Look, I may not have been the best father in the world. It may look like I brought Bobby here just to increase my odds on the deal. That's what Bobby thought. It's what his mother thought. But I'll tell you"—he looked away from me—"that was my way of getting him here, with me. He didn't understand any more than you do." Felcher's face was flushed. "I had this nice place for him, and he never brought a thing here. No magazines, not even a hairbrush. And, lady, no knife!" His fist smashed into the desk.

As if by reaction, the phone rang. Felcher snatched it up. "Yeah? What? Who? Oh, yeah."

He held out the phone to me.

"Hello?"

"Officer Smith, this is Heather Lee. You know, from the temple?"

"Yes, Heather. Why are you calling me here?"

"I called the police station. They told me where you were. It's important."

"I'm talking to someone."

"Well, this is important. You said something about not leaving town. Well, I have to go. I have to go tonight."

"You can't leave until the investigation is completed."

"I can't wait that long."

"Why?"

"Because of Chattanooga," she said with a triumphant finality.

"Chattanooga?"

"Yeah, Chattanooga Charlie Spotts. He's heading for Eureka to do a gig there. He wants me to go with him. He's going tonight."

"I'm sorry, Heather, but I can't let you leave Berkeley."

There was a noise as if she'd started to protest, then reconsidered. "You mean as soon as Padma's murder is solved I can go?"

"Right."

"Well, then, I think I can tell you who killed him."

"You know who the murderer is?"

"I think so."

"Well, who is it?"

"Wait. If I help you, will you get them to make sure I can leave right away? I won't be involved in anything about Padma not being a real guru, will I?"

"I'm sure something can be worked out."

"You're sure?"

"I said I was. Who killed him, Heather?"

I could hear her breathing. "I want to check on something. Meet me in an hour."

"Heather, where are you?"

"In the temple office."

"Is anyone there with you? Heather, you'd better tell me what you know now. It's dangerous to have that kind of secret. You don't know if someone's overheard you. You can hear a lot through that office window." I knew that from my own experience.

"No, I—"

"Heather, you could be killed."

She laughed. "Meet me in an hour. Meet me someplace real. You have an expense account, don't you? For informers?" She laughed again. "Meet me at Priester's, on the Avenue. I could use a hamburger."

"Heather—"

But the phone had gone dead. I stood staring at it, wondering if I could count on Heather's meeting me at Priester's restaurant. I'd meant to scare her, but recalling the ease with which I'd overheard Felcher and Braga's conversation in that room, I realized that what I'd told Heather was too true to be taken lightly.

I ran for my car.

Chapter 20

The rain had stopped temporarily, but dark clouds sagged down from the sky, intensifying the dim gray of dusk. Now, at five o'clock, the wet Berkeley streets looked like night.

Even with the flasher and siren on, it took me twenty minutes to get back to the temple. I raced down the steps to Braga's office. Empty. Up, through the door under the stage, into the temple proper. It held only a group of Penlops. Spotting me, they turned silent.

"Have you seen Heather in the last half hour?" I asked.

The blond Penlop spoke for the group. "No."

Running out the back door, I headed across the courtyard to the tepee and pulled the flap half open. The marble oil lamp was lit, but there was no sign of Heather. Only her matching leather suitcases stood there, lined up by the door, ready to go to Eureka.

The ashram was no better. Leah wasn't there. Two Penlops were asleep. Chupa-da's attic room was empty. I tried to think where else Heather could be. Maybe she'd found what she wanted and gone on to Priester's early.

I ran back to the car, headed through the one-way traffic on the Avenue and double-parked in front of the restaurant, ignoring the angry drivers behind me. Moving through the restaurant, I generated a fair amount of uneasiness among the customers but didn't find Heather.

If she was not at the temple, not in her tepee, not in the ashram, not here, where was she? Had someone overheard our conversation and got to her already?

There was no way to tell. There was no sense in staying here. If she made it to the restaurant, she'd be okay.

I walked back to the car, started to call in for the beat officers to watch for her, and realized I didn't know what she was wearing. The description I could give was so general as to fit a quarter of the girls on the Avenue.

I drove back to the temple, got out of the car and moved toward the dimly lit building. Forty-five minutes had passed since Heather's call. Anything could have happened.

If the murderer hadn't found her before my race through the buildings here, he could have after I'd left: And—I stopped in my steps—it wasn't only the crew here I had to worry about. I didn't know whether they'd heard what Heather had said, but I had repeated all the salient points with Vernon Felcher sitting right beside me. I'd announced where Heather was, what she knew and the fact that she was alone.

I moved slowly to the temple door.

A hand touched my shoulder.

I whirled.

Heather smiled. "You don't waste much time. But I want to go to Priester's."

I leaned back against the temple wall. "Where have you been? Are you all right? No one bothered you?"

"Yeah, sure. I'm fine. I just went to the all-night drugstore. You know that far-out rouge I had? Scintillatingly Scarlet, it's called. Well, I lost it and—"

"You held up a murder investigation to buy rouge?" The fury was evident in my voice.

Heather turned, stalked to the patrol car and treated me to an icy silence all the way to the restaurant. It wasn't till after we were seated and she had ordered herself a cheeseburger deluxe, their special salad and a Coke that she said, "Okay."

"So who's the killer?" I asked in a half whisper.

"Vernon Felcher, the real-estate man."

"Felcher!"

"Felcher. Yeah."

I leaned forward. "How do you know it was Felcher?"

"I don't *know*. I didn't say that I knew for sure. I just figured it out because everything points that way."

"What things?"

The waitress arrived with Heather's meal and my cup of coffee. Seeing the food, I wished I'd ordered something to eat, too.

"What things?" I repeated.

"Well, there's motive. I mean, he was Bobby's father. I can see where he'd be really pissed off that Bobby died in the ashram. I mean, as a mother, I can understand that. I mean, I can see where he might blame Paul."

I felt irritation setting in. "Any other motive?"

"Well, there's the land. I know he wants the land."

"Anything else?"

Heather strained to think. She obviously wanted to tell me enough to ensure her right to leave town. She would have personally placed Felcher before a firing squad if it would have reunited her with Chattanooga Charlie.

"Well," she said, "there are other things besides motive. I mean, he was right there."

"Where?"

"He was at the ceremony."

That was news. Felcher had told me he was at a movie. "Are you sure?"

"Yeah, Leah told me. I remember because I was surprised he'd have the gall to come, particularly on that night when there was so big a crowd they'd had to turn people away." She looked more confident now. Biting into the cheeseburger, she watched my reaction. My mouth was watering—one reaction.

"His being there doesn't prove he killed Paul," I informed her. "As a matter of fact, if he was in the audience it means that he was not under the stage. He was not in a position to knife Paul."

Heather chewed hurriedly. "No. Umm. Listen, Leah said he was sitting right up front. On the aisle just a couple of rows from her."

I remembered Leah deVeau, sitting in the front row. I remembered her lifting her hands to Padmasvana. "You're sure she said he was on the aisle?"

"Ye . . . yes, I'm sure."

I sipped my coffee, barely aware of the taste. "Heather, I still don't see how that implicates him. If he'd gotten up, walked to the back of the room, out and around to the basement steps, through the basement to the trapdoor, to—"

"No. Umm." She put up a hand and swallowed quickly. "He didn't have to do that. That's the point. He would be right by the door under the stage. All he had to do was slip through there, pop up through the trapdoor, plunge the knife and sit back down."

"Don't you think that would have been rather obvious?"

"Jesus! Don't you remember what that room was like? I looked in once or twice during the ceremony. Felcher could have set off a firecracker and no one would have noticed."

I lifted the coffee cup halfway and held it. Heather had a point. Felcher could have slipped through the stage door, killed Paul and, in the ensuing panic, slipped back into his seat. People had jumped up; they'd screamed; one or two had fainted. It would have been no problem at all to melt into the swarming crowd. Even Felcher, an outsider, would have had no trouble. And, likely, he had access to the murder weapon.

There was one problem with this theory, of course. The Penlops at the door had sworn no one had left the building or grounds after the stabbing, and Felcher had not been on our list of people in the audience. Still, I supposed he could have been there and managed to sneak away somehow.

"Anything else?" I asked as Heather started in on her salad.

"What more do you need!"

"Then that's it?"

"Yeah. Isn't it enough? Can't I go? Chattanooga will be leaving."

"I can't let you go until we have an arrest. It could be soon, or maybe not. Get Chattanooga's schedule and meet him along the way. If it's true love," I said with a straight face, "it will survive."

"Shit!"

Ignoring my suggestions to hurry, Heather dallied over her salad, ordered a slice of banana-cream pie and, finally, announced that she would get home alone. I reminded her that Felcher was loose and that, if what she implied were true, he could be dangerous. Heather was not impressed. She'd walk back along the Avenue, under the streetlights. At the temple there'd be people. She'd be okay, she assured me. And anyway, she kind of knew this guy a couple of booths down and she wanted to say hello and . . .

Reiterating my warning, I left and drove back across town to Comfort Realty.

The building was dark. Felcher was gone. How soon after Heather's call had he left? Had he kept the appointment with his unidentified caller? Or had his need to find Heather pre-empted that?

Hurrying back to the car, I drove to Felcher's apartment in the hills by the Kensington city line. It was the bottom unit of a duplex and it, too, was dark. I banged on the door to the upper unit. Irritated, a middle-aged woman shuffled down to the door and responded that no, she had not heard Felcher tonight. No, that was not unusual; he rarely came home before eleven. Yes, she was sure he hadn't been there. She's been watching a movie on television—one that she was now missing—and she would have had no trouble hearing Felcher's car.

Could Felcher have left town? Should I alert the airports, the bus depots and the Santa Fe station? Was he somewhere on I-5 headed south? Or driving madly toward the open spaces of Nevada or speeding north for the Oregon line?

Or was he hiding around the ashram, waiting for Heather?

I turned the car, put on the pulsers and raced back down the hill, calling in an all-points to the Highway Patrol on the way.

It was almost seven o'clock. I called in again to ask for backup as I pulled the patrol car up in front of the temple.

Shutting the car door quietly, I started across the court-yard. Footsteps hit the walkway behind me.

I turned.

"Heather!" I stopped. "This is the second time tonight you've done that."

"Done what?"

"Never mind. I'm just glad you're all right."

"I'm *not* all right. I'm lousy! Chattanooga Charlie's already left. Someone at Priester's saw him pack up. He didn't even tell me he was going. He didn't even bother."

Her face drooped. The scowl that usually marked it was

replaced by a genuinely woebegone expression. For the first time, I felt some sympathy for Heather, some sense of kinship. I put my hand on her shoulder. "Come on, maybe it'll help to talk about it." It wouldn't hurt for me to sit in the tepee until the backup crew arrived and listen. I'd run out of nearby places to look for Vernon Felcher, anyway.

Heather nodded, and together we walked across the courtyard. She lifted the tepee flap, stepped inside and screamed.

Chapter 21

There on the floor amid broken makeup bottles lay Vernon Felcher. The back of his head was caved in. His blood had stained the bottles and streaked the white paint on the table as he slid down. There was blood on his jacket, blood on what I could see of his face. And there was blood on the marble lamp, lying beside Felcher's body.

Pushing Heather outside, I followed, inhaling deeply, trying to control my nausea. Heather leaned against the tepee and retched. I took another breath and started across the courtyard to my car radio.

As I reached it, the backup crew I'd called for arrived. I told them. "It's a one-eighty-seven—bludgeoned with a marble lamp. Outgrowth of the guru stabbing here Wednesday."

"Your case?"

"Yeah."

He nodded with a touch of disappointment. Of course, he hadn't seen Vernon Felcher's body. He hadn't known Felcher alive. "I'll run logistics: you want to take the suspects, since you know who they are?"

"Right. Thanks."

In another ten minutes the courtyard was alive with lights, aswarm with uniforms. The photographer and the print man arrived and headed for the tepee. The Penlops were herded into the dining room for questioning, their formerly glazed countenances now sullenly angry. One backup man went to find Braga, two more covered Joe Lee and Leah. And one drove off to keep an eye on Garrett Kleinfeld.

Another had taken Heather to my car. She was sitting stiffly in the back seat when I arrived. I glanced at the patrolman, but he shook his head to indicate nothing worth reporting had happened.

I slid in beside Heather. "How are you holding up?"

"I don't know," she said. "I keep seeing him, with his blood spattered all over my bed and my dressing table and my suitcase and my clothes." Her hand tightened on her knee.

"Heather," I said, "I want you to tell me exactly what happened tonight when you called me, and after."

She shook her head. "What do you mean? I called you."

"From Braga's office, right?"

"Yes."

"Did you notice anyone outside the window?"

"No. I mean, I didn't look. You know, I really wasn't thinking about that. I mean, I just decided to call you. I had to put all my energy on that. It wasn't easy to get the police station to tell me where you were. I had to tell them it was life or death."

Her voice trailed off, and we both sat silent for a moment, thinking of the prophetic value of her words.

"Then what did you do?"

"I met you and went to the restaurant."

"Before that."

"I told you, I bought the rouge. Do you want to see the sales slip?"

"That's great, really great, Heather. You realize if you

hadn't waited that hour, we would have got back here sooner and Vernon Felcher wouldn't be dead."

"You can't blame me! I didn't ask him to get murdered in my tepee. That's my home. Where am I going to sleep tonight? What about my suitcases? And my clothes? This is the thanks I get for trying to help you!"

I *had* overreacted, but an apology did not seem called for. I sighed. "Vernon Felcher overheard enough of our conversation to know what you'd told me. Why do you think he came here?"

She thought a moment, then shuddered. "He overheard, and he came to my tepee? He must have been after me."

"Wait. You didn't say you suspected him then. You said that later. Then, you only said you knew who the killer was. So, if Vernon Felcher didn't stab Paul—and the odds are now that he didn't—why would he come here?"

When Heather didn't answer, I asked, "Was it to see you?"

"What? No. I told you I didn't see anyone. Why would Felcher want to see me?"

"He might want to know what you knew. He might have been worried about you."

She laughed. "I doubt that. He wasn't interested in anything but land."

I considered that. "Okay, Heather, after I left you at the restaurant, what did you do till you came back here?"

"I talked to this guy for a while. You know, the one I told you about. He's kind of a strange guy, but he's a great dancer. He's—"

"Heather!"

"Okay, I was with him about ten minutes. I would have stayed longer, but he had his old lady with him, and she was getting very uptight and finally she stood up and made a big deal about wanting to split. So I left and came back here."

"I'll need his name and address."

"Okay. I can give you his name—Bill Katz. I don't know for sure where he lives. Somewhere around the Avenue. Now can I go? I might be able to catch Chattanooga in Eureka."

"What?"

"Can I go now?"

"Heather," I said, slamming my note pad shut, "don't even think about leaving town. You've already handed me this line about knowing who the killer was—"

"I didn't say I knew. What I told you was true. Felcher was in the temple. He could have slipped through the stage door. He could have done it."

"Or you could have. Twenty-five percent of murders are committed by the victim's husband or wife."

She glared at me, her long sandy hair vibrating with her rage. "I wasn't Paul's wife, if that's what you mean."

"Close enough. You're the mother of his child."

"No."

"No?"

"I'm not the mother of his child."

I took a breath. This case had been filled with false representations—Paul Lee had not been a guru; the insignia on the murder weapon had not been a Buddhist or Bhutanese symbol—but this was too much for me to accept. "Heather, I can't believe you're not Preston's mother."

She shook her head in disgust. "Of course I'm his mother. But Paul wasn't his father."

Before I could ask, she added, "Joe."

"I didn't think she'd ever admit it." Joe Lee sat back in his desk chair in the attic room. "Yeah, I'm Preston's father."

"Didn't you mind everyone thinking Paul was his father?"

"Yeah, I minded. Of course I minded. It wasn't my idea.

All of a sudden Heather was telling everyone that. And Paul didn't care. That was at the time he was beginning to get into being guru. He said something about everyone being fathers to everyone else."

"And you did nothing?"

"What could I do? Who would have believed me?"

"There are blood tests."

"Paul's and mine were the same type."

"So you did nothing."

"Right."

"Maybe there was more to your inaction than resignation?" When he didn't respond, I added, "Maybe you saw an advantage to having your son in a position to be Padmasvana's successor. Maybe you figured that with him dead, even if you didn't succeed him, your son could."

He started to speak, but I held up a hand. "Maybe you realized that if Heather was the regent, she would have that role in name only; that you would be the power behind the throne."

"You through? Forget it. You'd love to pin this murder on me, on a Chinese. I suppose you think I stuck on a braid and made like the tong wars."

"You're not answering my question."

His short hair bristled. "Yeah, I'm no fool. I thought of the advantages. *After* Paul was dead. I did not kill my brother."

"And Felcher?"

He snorted. "Why would I bother killing that old man?"

"For starters, because with Paul dead, you had a good chance of taking over. Unless Felcher bought the land. Then Braga would get the money, and you would be out with nothing. You had a lot to lose if Felcher had lived."

Joe Lee smirked, a definitely unpleasant expression. "And Braga's got a lot to lose now," he said. "Oh, yeah, I know about his debts to his 'friends' in L.A. What'll he tell them when his time's up?"

If I had any delusions about a bond between Braga and Joe Lee, they were gone. Had Joe, I wondered, thought he could throw Braga to the wolves—to his bloodthirsty creditors—by killing Felcher?

"Where were you tonight? For the last two hours?"

The smirk disappeared. "Right here. Ask the Penlops. They'll tell you."

"You'd better come up with a stronger alibi than that. The days of the Penlops obeying you are over."

"No, I didn't see Chupa-da—Joe—leave," Leah said. "Of course, I wouldn't have. I was in the basement. There are washtubs down there. I was washing out some diapers." She glanced at Preston, sleeping in his basket. This was a new variety of alibi.

"I have to wash them out," Leah explained. "It would be easier to use the disposable ones, but I can't spend the boys' food money just to save me work."

"Why were you washing so late?"

"I had just realized that diapers had run out. I knew I'd need some the next day. Since Padma's death, my hours have become a bit irregular."

"Did you see anyone that night? Maybe you looked out through the basement window and saw someone?"

"No."

"Vernon Felcher? Maybe you saw him hanging around outside?"

She laughed, then stopped abruptly. "I'm sorry. It's just that Vernon Felcher was such a pushy man and yet he was truly squeamish about being outside. The man had some sort of allergy—you know how those people are? They worry about anything that grows. And, to answer your question, I didn't see him or anyone else that night."

"So, then, no one can verify that you were in the basement that night, either?"

She shook her head.

Outside, I could hear the angry grumblings of Penlops who were waiting to be questioned.

"Leah," I continued, "according to Heather, you did see Vernon Felcher in the audience the night that Paul was killed."

She nodded.

"You and Heather agreed that he could have gone through the door under the stage and up through the trapdoor to kill Paul. In all that commotion he could have gone through the door unnoticed, right?"

"It's awful. I didn't like the man, but it's just awful to think that."

"But it *is* possible?"

"Yes."

"Then it would have been possible for you to do the same thing."

Her eyes opened wider. She stared at me silently. She shook her head. "You can't mean that? Me? Kill Paul?" She shrank back, and I felt truly distressed that I had mentioned the possibility. Again, I reminded myself that criminals were not always those easily labeled as such.

"It would have been easier for you than for Felcher. You had on a red robe. You were so much a part of the operation here that you could move about unnoticed. If anyone did see you, they would have recalled a figure in a red robe, a Penlop robe. In the dark they wouldn't have associated it particularly with you."

She sat, shaking her head.

I felt like a class-A heel. Did I really think Leah had killed

Paul? Could she have seen Felcher as the ultimate threat to the ashram? Was she unbalanced enough to kill him in a vain attempt to keep the house for her boys? I couldn't believe that. The motive was too thin.

There was nothing more to say. I stood up slowly and walked across the courtyard.

Rexford Braga sat slumped behind his desk. He didn't look up when I entered the office.

"Did you get a statement?" I asked the patrolman.

"He hasn't said anything. I understood I was to wait for you."

"Fine."

He looked at me questioningly, silently asking if he were being relieved. I shook my head. "I won't be long." To Braga, I said, "Where were you tonight?"

He continued to stare at the desk.

"Mr. Braga?"

Still no movement. This was certainly not the Braga I was used to. What event could be so earthshaking as to reduce Braga to silence? Felcher's murder? I doubted it.

I sat on the desk, in his line of vision. "What did you do after five tonight?"

He looked up, glowering. "What difference does it make? Leave me alone."

"As soon as you answer my questions."

"Oh, all right. I was driving around, alone, all evening. I've got a lot to think about."

"Anyone see you?"

"I doubt it."

"No alibi, then?"

"Look, if you don't believe me, put me in jail. It doesn't matter."

"What are you taking so hard?"

"Felcher's dead."

Sarcastically, I said, "I didn't think you cared so much."

"Care?" He looked up, genuinely surprised. "I don't give a damn about Felcher. I care about my hundred thou. You know where this leaves me? I've got a little more than a month to come up with a hundred thou."

"But you still own the property. Maybe some other realtor will want the land."

Braga shook his head. "The variance runs out in ten days, and it's not transferable, anyway."

Motioning to the patrolman, I left Braga with his dilemma.

Chapter 22

I walked slowly back to my car. The rain still held off, but the wind raked the trees.

If Felcher had not come in search of Heather, then he had been lured to the tepee by the killer—in the call that I overheard in his office, the one after which he had said the laundry had lost his shirt. At the time, his conversation with the unknown caller had seemed to echo something else I'd heard recently. "Don't give me that self-sacrificing crap again. Look, I'm in the middle of negotiating a deal, I don't have time . . ." And who would want Felcher killed in the tepee? Who would benefit by Felcher's death? Not Braga, certainly. He would only lose the money he could have made on the land. Where *would* Felcher's money go? His son was dead. Felcher didn't seem the sort to leave it to his ex-wife. I could go through his office to find his lawyer's name, but it was now after nine on Saturday night, and the lawyer might well be out. Trying to get information from a lawyer without a warrant is a small-percentage proposition at the best of times.

Who would benefit?

Going with the odds, I headed toward Self-Over.

Garrett Kleinfeld and a new man on my shift, Martinez, whom I knew from a case several months ago, sat silently against the wall. As I walked in, Martinez scrambled to his feet. He extended his notes.

"Not much," he said, and yawned.

I read through the page of half-words and symbols, some familiar and some I had to have Martinez interpret. When I handed him back the notebook, he took me aside and said, "Listen, Smith, I have had one hard shift. I really need coffee. Like this guy could have walked over me on the way out and I would have shrugged, you know?"

"Okay, take ten. But either way, I'll need you then."

"Sure." He ambled to the door.

Garrett Kleinfeld watched Martinez's retreating form with disdain. For me he chose an expression of long suffering, of a man stretched nearly to breaking point.

"So you say you've been here all evening?" I asked.

"That's what the man wrote."

"Doing exercises? All evening?"

"Right again." The lines around his mouth stretched downward. "You want to see?" he demanded.

Before I could protest, he wrapped his feet around his back so that he resembled a turtle balanced on the back edge of its shell.

"Sit up," I said. "I don't have time for show-and-tell. I want some answers, and I want them now."

He unwound himself and sat.

I squatted in front of him.

"Now that Felcher's dead, do you inherit the rights to the building?"

Kleinfeld stared, then almost laughed. "Obviously you don't understand Vernon Felcher."

"Fine. Then you tell me about him and what plans he made for the disposition of his property."

"I don't know that!"

"Come on, Mr. Kleinfeld. Felcher was middle-aged, overweight. He ticked like a time bomb. Don't tell me you never considered that he might die."

"Well, I . . ."

"You . . . ?" I prodded.

"Yeah, okay. I thought about it. It's written into his will that if he dies before the building is completed and the tenants take occupancy, the first floor will be mine."

"For how much?"

Kleinfeld appeared to wage a brief and futile battle against the smug expression that took possession of his face. "For free."

"For how long?"

"As long as the building stands. It'll be like owning a condominium. When I move on, I'll rent the space."

I leaned back against the wall. "So, Mr. Kleinfeld, Vernon Felcher's death would not only save you money, but would give you a security you could never count on with him alive."

Kleinfeld said nothing.

"Except for the fact that he had not completed the deal for the land. Or didn't you know that?"

The smug expression hardened into a mask.

Rolling onto the balls of my feet, I said, "Vernon Felcher was killed on the temple grounds. That appears to implicate everyone involved in this case, except you. Very convenient."

I waited.

Kleinfeld remained motionless.

"He got a call from his murderer, to arrange the meeting. Tonight, when you were alone, exercising." I let the sarcasm ring through.

Kleinfeld still sat behind his mask, but he had an air of coiling inward.

"Vernon Felcher said to the killer, 'Don't give me that self-sacrificing crap again. I'm—' "

"Wait! And you thought he was talking to *me?*"

Now I waited.

"Well, that just shows how little you comprehended about what I've told you. No wonder the crime rate in Berkeley's what it is, if this is the level of police we have. Self-sacrifice! That's what I'm working against. That's what I tell my students. There are too many goddamn martyrs. What they need is to lift the self up. To the Self first—not to be a slave to anyone else. Self-Over. *Over!*"

I had to admit to myself that the concept of Kleinfeld sacrificing was a hard one to see. Suddenly I remembered what Felcher's words had reminded me of—it was almost exactly what I'd said when I thought I was talking to Nat on the phone yesterday: "I'm in the middle of a murder case, I don't have time to . . ." And Felcher had said, "I'm in the middle of negotiating a deal. I don't have time to . . ." The same, down to the exasperated tone. And now I didn't have time to think through the implications.

I asked, "What about Bobby's knife? Did he really take it away from here?"

"What? Of course."

"Do you have any proof? Do you have more than your word?"

"You don't believe me! What's the sense in talking? Jesus!" He grabbed my arm.

Twisting it free and jumping up, I said, "You lied before. I need proof. Were there any witnesses?"

"I don't—"

"Were there any witnesses?"

"Yes, there were witnesses. There was a whole class. They heard the argument."

"I'll need their names and addresses."

"I can't give you that!" His hands curled into fists; he took a breath, struggling for control. I remembered him saying that he had almost killed a man once, in a rage.

Fighting my impulse to back away, I held my ground. "The names."

"I don't know the names. I don't remember who was in every class. I'd have to get in touch with every student I've had."

"Fine."

"Are you telling me to go through every class list, to call every student, to—"

"That's what I'm telling you."

His hands locked around my wrists. "Look, I'm saying this for the last time: Bobby Felcher left here with that knife. He took it home."

Jerking loose, I said, "He didn't take it to Felcher's."

"Then maybe he took it to his mother's, or the ashram." His face was white, his body poised to attack.

"I'll check it out." I headed for the door.

Chapter 23

In that rage, Kleinfeld could have done anything. With my department training, I could have held him off, but it might have meant using my gun.

I sat back in the patrol car, half listening to the squeals from the radio. I had hoped to find out something definite about Bobby's knife. As of now, I had only Kleinfeld's word that the knife had ever left the Self-Over studio. But if it had, what were the options? Could Bobby have brought it into the ashram concealed among his belongings? There had been no housemother then. I couldn't picture Braga or Joe Lee searching every Penlop as he entered. I started the car and headed toward the ashram.

I drove quickly through dark glistening streets. I could feel the answers dancing at the edge of my brain, waiting for the right place to alight.

I needed to think, to sit someplace quiet, someplace where I could mull over the case undisturbed.

I pulled up the car outside the temple and hurried across the walk to the door. It was open. Inside, it was dark except for the candles on the altar under the big picture of Padmasvana. I stood, accustoming my eyes to the dimness, then moved halfway down the aisle and sat.

Looking up at the benevolent expression in the picture, I

wondered what I expected it to tell me. What did I think I would find in this phony temple? Had the knife been in here all along?

Bobby Felcher had died more than a year ago. After his death, the department had turned the temple and ashram inside out looking for drugs. If the knife had been here, it would have been found. It would have been mentioned in the report, along with the gun Braga kept downstairs in his desk drawer.

Then had Bobby taken the knife to his mother's? He'd spent every other weekend with her. Should I contact the Visalia police—have them check out Elizabeth Felcher? Would she still live in Visalia? Would she remember what her son had kept in his room nearly two years ago? Whatever, it was certainly going to take the case well past the Sunday morning deadline set by Lt. Davis.

I slumped back on the seat. Felcher—the key had to be Vernon Felcher. Any of them could have killed Paul Lee, but why kill Felcher?

I came up with no new answers. Padmasvana's picture smiled down at me.

Three murders—Bobby Felcher, Paul Lee, Vernon Felcher. Leah, Joe and Heather witnessed Paul placing his confession in the strongbox. Vern—and therefore Kleinfeld if he were interested—was sure Paul killed Bobby. So they were all sure Paul killed Bobby, killed him competently, almost in a businesslike manner, just as he himself was killed. Bobby and Paul, disposed of.

But Vern Felcher was different. This death was a crime of vengeance.

Who hated him enough to smash a lamp into his head again and again, till it caved in his skull? Who—The candles went out. The room was black. "Who's there? What are you doing?" I looked at the stage, but I could make out nothing.

"Who are you? How did you get up there?"

No answer. But there was only one way anyone could have got there without my noticing—through the trapdoor. Someone had come into the basement, moved quietly past Braga's office and come up through the trapdoor under the altar.

"Who are you? What do you want?"

Footsteps broke the silence. Instinctively, I crouched down. Only a faint light from the windows diminished the blackness. I could barely see two rows in front of me.

Feet smacked to the floor. Whoever it was had jumped from the stage. He—or she—was down here with me.

"Who are you?"

In the silence, I heard a click—the gun Braga kept in his drawer?

"Is that you, Braga?"

Still, the silence. Stooping, I slithered between the rows of seats, moving slowly, trying to keep my leather shoes from squeaking on the cement floor. I thought longingly of the doors—the one to the basement and the main one—but once I opened either, any light behind them would outline me. I would make an easy target for the killer.

My mind raced: the knife, Felcher's allergy; the phone call and Felcher's exasperation as he said, "Don't give me that self-sacrificing crap again." The exasperation that comes from years of . . . self-sacrifice.

Taking a breath, I said, "I know who you are. I know why you killed them."

Feet shuffled, feet in rubber-soled shoes. They had moved down the aisle, halfway to the door.

"You called Felcher tonight. You got him to the tepee and smashed his head in."

I waited. Silence.

"You hit him again and again. You paid him back for his greed, his neglect."

The footsteps moved toward me. I slid farther down between the seats. "You planted the story about Felcher being in the temple when Paul was killed."

I waited, aware that I was pinpointing my location with my voice. More softly I said, "There were a couple of things wrong with that story. Felcher wouldn't have been familiar with Padmasvana's routine. He wouldn't have known when Padmasvana faced the altar. He wouldn't have known when to be there. And Felcher wasn't on our list of people in the audience. But you knew Padmasvana's routine. You had seen the ceremonies, time and time again."

Footsteps came from the direction of the altar. My hand jerked to my holster, poised. I couldn't talk and listen, too. But I needed to have the killer make a move.

"As soon as he learned from me that you were the housemother, Felcher began to suspect you'd killed Paul because of Bobby. That's why he turned up and all but accused you at that memorial ceremony. And once he realized what the murder weapon was, he was sure . . .

The breeze tickled my neck. The prayer wheels swished in the forced air. There were no more footsteps.

"Paul killed Bobby, and then he was ready to abandon the temple. Felcher sent Bobby here to be killed and then he planned to wipe out the temple—to destroy the only thing that remained in your life."

The footsteps moved in. They were about five rows away, close enough for even a bad shot to hit me.

"Felcher, who *you* told me was allergic—"

The gun fired.

The bang resounded. The flash lit the room.

I ran, leaped on the squatting body, pushing it down. I hit out against the arms. The gun clattered to the floor.

Panting, I said, "Okay, Leah."

Chapter 24

Handcuffing Leah to the leg of the altar table and leaving her to consider the rights I had just read her, I called the station. I could have questioned her there, but somehow the end had to come here, in the temple.

Leah appeared quite calm when I got back. I adjusted the handcuffs and sat across from her on a pillow. Above us the giant picture of Padmasvana fluttered in the breeze from the fans. Oblivious of human concerns, the prayer wheels rotated.

"Leah, I know you are Elizabeth deVeau."

She looked up, surprised.

"You slipped and left that name when you called me at the station. And I know you're also Elizabeth Felcher, Vernon's ex-wife, Bobby's mother. Was deVeau your maiden name?"

She nodded.

"You pretended not to know Felcher, but you were the one who told me about his allergies. You described your ex-husband well enough for me to see the connection to the man with terrible hay fever whose sneezing made so much noise.

She nodded again but made no move to speak. "Bobby brought the knife to your house in Visalia, the place he thought of as home. Did you bring it here to kill Paul?"

"No!" She shuddered, as if startled by the sound of her

own voice. "Well, not specifically. I guess unconsciously I did plan to use it. But I didn't even know Paul was the killer. I wasn't sure until I saw him put the confession in the strongbox." She pushed a shock of gray hair out of her face. "Oh, I knew Bobby had been murdered. I knew it wasn't a simple overdose because of his fear of needles, but I didn't consciously come here to kill."

I said nothing, and I could tell from her eyes that she was moving into herself, speaking for the relief it brought. I was fading into the background for her.

"I came to Berkeley to see where Bobby died, really, just to see. I needed that, to grieve for that portion of his life I'd had no part in. Or that's what I thought. I was fooling myself; I know that, now." She pulled her knees up to her chest, wrapping her arms around them. Despite her gray hair and that face that could never have been pretty, she looked, in the pale light of the altar, like a young girl talking about things she only half understood.

"I knew Bobby hadn't overdosed—because of the needle. I wanted to go to the police, but Vern convinced me—he always convinced me—it would do no good. He convinced me I would just look like a hysterical middle-aged woman.

"So I came to Berkeley. I realized that the person who murdered Bobby had to be someone in the temple. The Penlops' lives were too circumscribed for an outsider to be able to wander in, give a boy some drug, wait for it to work and then . . ." Her voice quavered, but she forced the words out. "And then push a needle in his arm. I realized that, but still, I probably would have gone back to Visalia, certain there was nothing I could do.

"But then, my first night in Berkeley, I saw an ad. The temple was looking for a housemother. For some reason, when I applied I gave my maiden name." She half shrugged and leaned back against the altar, as if the rest were obvious.

I said, "But you were here quite a while before you killed Paul."

She looked up, surprised; she had nearly forgotten I was here. "At first I wanted revenge right away, but I didn't know which of them killed Bobby. I considered killing them all, but"—she stared directly at me as if soliciting reassurance—"I'm not a ghoul. I'm not crazy. So I waited, gathering evidence. But I wasn't sure it was Paul till he wrote that confession he put in the strongbox. He just slapped it in there. I could barely keep silent! He put it in there and they watched. Bobby didn't matter to any of them! He was no more than a piece of paper they could use to control each other."

"And?"

"Then I had to decide on the time and the place."

"And you killed Vernon because he sent Bobby here?"

"Yes." The word was barely audible.

For a motive, it was plenty, but somehow not enough. "Leah," I said, "other people have had sons killed and not killed in return. You don't seem like a violent person. You don't live by 'an eye for an eye . . .' "

She looked up with an expression of gratitude. "No. It wasn't just for Bobby. It was for me, too. It's funny. Being housemother was something I was good at. It's the first real job I've had. I've been through bad times—when Vernon left, when I learned of Bobby's death. I've had nothing, no family, barely enough to live on, nothing to hope for. I thought about suicide—many times—and then I took this job. I succeeded here. I was needed. I was doing something important."

"And then Paul was going to leave and take all that away."

"Yes, and then Vernon. He sent Bobby here to die, and then because he could make money, he was going to toss the other boys onto the street. And me with them."

"And?"

"Well, after I'd killed Paul, killing wasn't foreign to me. It's rather like having your first auto accident." She smiled wanly. "I called Vern—he tried to put me off—but I told him, definitely, like I'd never done before, to meet me in the tepee—and he came. He knew I'd killed Paul, of course, because of Bobby's knife, but Paul's death suited him, so he kept quiet. He was closer to getting the property." She laughed. "I guess Vern figured the city wouldn't like his getting rich because his ex-wife killed someone.

"Anyway, he stomped into the tepee like he already owned the property. He demanded—like he'd done all those years! He'd taken my youth, my son, and now what little I'd been able to scrape together to pass as a life he was ready to kick aside without even seeing it. I picked up the lamp and brought those years down on his head." She hesitated, then said softly, "You see, don't you, why it was so much easier to kill him."

I stood up, looking away from the eyes that beseeched me to understand.

"I'm sorry," she said. She was staring at my forehead, at the bruise. "Not about them, about that. But I did have to hit you, to keep you from searching Mr. Braga's office and finding the box with Padma's note. I saw Padma write that note, but I never knew where Mr. Braga kept the strongbox. I just assumed it would be in his office. And if you found the note and started making connections . . ." Her voice trailed off.

Then, looking up, she added, "I did leave the light on, so you wouldn't be lying on Mr. Braga's floor in the dark."

There'd been the usual—photographs, fingerprints, Leah

deVeau's formal statement. And there'd been the press, the report to Lt. Davis, the questions from the other beat men: no one goes home at 11:00 p.m. when a murder is cleared up; everyone wants the word first hand. And normally I would have been delighted to give it.

But now I just felt tired. And sad.

When the others had cleared out and the nightshift men had torn themselves away to cruise their beats, Howard was still in my chair.

"You're beginning to look like a fixture there," I said.

He grinned. "Maybe you won't be needing it now. This has been a big case to break. Like I told you, it'll look good on your record. It was good experience."

Thinking of Leah and of Vern Felcher and of Paul Lee lying in front of the altar, I said, "Maybe, but it's not a pleasant way to climb."

"Still . . ."

Looking down at Howard, at the abnormal seriousness of his face, I realized it was a sacrifice for him to discuss the advantage I had gained while I made little of it. I lopped off a chunk from my lump of trust and said, "Thanks. Buy you a drink?"

Now the grin returned. "Just one?"

"No, not just one."

He stood up. "And tomorrow, after you've read the newspaper reports of your derring-do, Officer Smith, what are you going to do to celebrate?"

I glanced down at my stack of unanswered phone messages. "The first thing is to go to Cost Plus and buy a set of their best stainless."